ANTHONY J SANTORA

THE GUIDED

A Nathan Turner Story

PRIVATE DRAGON
Publishing

First edition

ISBN: 978-1-951405-25-0

Editing by Jake Lueckler
Cover art by Samantha Knight

This book was professionally typeset on Reedsy.
Find out more at reedsy.com

Contents

Prologue

Ever since I was a child, I've seen things that others couldn't. This sight has been a curse on my life and has cost me everything. I have no family, no home, and no connection to this world. A large part of me wants to end my life, but I know how those that kill themselves end up... I see them. Yes, I can sometimes see the dead, but that is the least of what I see. I see shadows and light everywhere and attached to everyone. There is what I can only describe as an essence that emanates from every person's head. I learned very early in my life that this light or darkness directly reflected the person it was attached to so that I could tell who was good and who was to be avoided. I guess most would consider this a gift, and maybe if that was all I saw it would be okay, but that is not all I see. All my life I've seen figures of light and shadow moving through the world. They hover around all of us, but I do not know why. Sometimes I'll see a sparkling explosion like fireworks when the light and dark touch each other. This is all happening in our world, everywhere, but nobody knows. I do not know what these things are, but there are a few things I've figured out. I feel comforted, and at peace whenever I'm around the light or a person whose light shines brightly, and I feel great fear, anger, and sadness around the dark, and there is far more dark. All my life I've seen these things as dark or light clouds with no distinct shape or form, but something has changed. The forms have begun to take shape into something more corporeal. I am beginning to see definition in the shadows, and I have never been more afraid.

   –Anne

Chapter 1: The Chosen

Anne walked down a busy street in New Orleans, trying to keep her eyes fixed on the ground a few feet in front of her as to avoid the shadows everywhere. It was midday, but that made no difference. The shadows she was avoiding didn't care what time it was. It would have been easy to not notice Anne as she would have blended in with any of the nearby homeless easily. She was actually a very beautiful young woman of nineteen with flowing red curly hair, piercing green eyes, and freckles, but the layer of grime and dirt on her mismatched clothes made her look like a user which garnered a lot of unwanted offers from drug dealers, pimps and the occasional well-to-do businessman looking to *help* her. It was times like that she was thankful for her gift of discernment. Of all the men who approached her, it was the well-dressed upscale ones that had the most darkness in them.

In truth, Anne had never used any illicit substances. The only medication she had ever taken was what was forced onto her by doctors in a mental health facility she was forcibly taken to after telling a counselor about the things she saw. The darkness in that place tormented her daily, and she swore she'd never tell another person of her sight ever again. Anne's chastity too had never been broken although many had tried through coercion or force. It wasn't a sense of morality that kept Anne from a physical relationship. It was her sight that made any relationship nearly impossible.

Anne hated big cities as the darkness in them seemed to infect the air she breathed, but they were also the only places for a homeless person to find food and shelter while remaining inconspicuous. Like most cities, New Orleans was loud and smelly. The smells in New Orleans however were many and distinct.

Anne had just followed a group of feet across the crosswalk when a smell so strong caught her attention and forced her nose up. She hadn't been in New Orleans long enough to know what food each aroma came from, and she certainly hadn't been able to eat at the finest restaurants. She looked at the chalkboard sign in front of the door.

Lunch Special

Shrimp and Sausage Jambalaya
  $6.99

Anne rummaged through her pockets to find $3.48.

"Halfway there," she whispered aloud, thinking she'd keep this place in mind as she tried to find the remaining cost.

At that moment, a couple came out of the restaurant and turned to walk down the sidewalk. A tall, stocky man and a short strawberry blonde with glasses. Their light pulsed brightly as she wrapped her arm around his and he kissed her head. Anne smiled to herself as she watched the happy couple walk away with two human-like forms of light following. She continued her walk down the street, this time with her head up looking around, although she occasionally scanned the ground for any change.

The sight she saw was a familiar one. All around her were people, their lights a varying shade of bright or dark. Most people were dimly lit by one or the other, but some, like the couple from the restaurant, lit brightly. Anne continued to walk and was pleased to hear a Zydeco band playing up ahead. As she made her way closer to the creole music, a light-skinned black man with a kango hat and freckles similar to hers greeted her with a smile as he passed by.

"Aight there, baaaby."

Getting used to the way people in New Orleans speak had been a bit of a challenge for Anne. In this case, for instance, many might think the man to be harassing or catcalling, but Anne's experience and the bright light emanating from the man's head told her he was just saying hello. Anne smiled and nodded as she passed the man and the zydeco band looking for her lunch money but enjoying the atmosphere.

As she was walking Anne saw a flash indicating that dark and light entities had clashed. She looked to her left to see a boy of maybe six and his mom waiting for the upcoming streetcar to arrive. They were both facing away. The mother holding her son's hand. The figure of light was there for a moment, then was gone instantly. The boy and his mother both had a very deep darkness. Anne had rarely seen such darkness in a child, but when she did, they were almost always accompanied by a parent with the same darkness.

Anne felt sad as she focused on the boy. Two dark shapes stood next to the mother and son and as she looked more intently, she saw the shadowy figure next to the boy begin to take shape. The forms taking shape had been new to her and she had been trying to not look at them directly, but she couldn't look away this time. She had to know what darkness was attached to this little boy.

Anne focused on the dark entity more intently, and as she did, the cloud of fog surrounding it began to coalesce. The more she focused, the clearer the being became until it was no longer composed of shadow and mist but flesh and bone. What Anne saw was unlike anything she had seen before. It had its back to her but was terrifying, nonetheless. It had dark rotting skin over muscled shoulders and arms. Its back was covered in a type of horned spikes that seemed to have pierced and broken through the skin, leaving a trail of puss and blood oozing down its back. There were both new and old slash marks covering the entirety of its body as if it had been punished. While its top was muscular, its lower ribs and waist were emaciated to the point of seeing the creature's organs through its thin skin. Its hips were unnatural and jutted out like armor over its thick and muscled legs. The calves elongated similar to a dog's, but the feet were that of some great horned predatory bird with talons that seemed to dig into the sidewalk.

As Anne looked at the monstrosity before her, the boy turned his head to meet her gaze as if he could sense her watching. He looked at her with the most hate-filled eyes she had ever seen, and then the beast too turned to look at her.

It had no ears to speak of, but dark pits placed where they might have been. There were two rows of boned protrusions above the eyes that trailed to the back of the head, but it had no hair. Although its brow, cheek, and chin bones were pronounced it retained a humanlike face but its eyes...

As the demon met eyes with Anne, she could see the black void in its eyes, but something was shining in them, not through them. A flame of hate, despair, fear, loathing could all be seen in its eyes, but then its eyes held another feeling, surprise. The demon's eyes widened as he realized this human could see him.

Anne's curiosity turned to fear instantly as she quickly averted her gaze and began quickly walking away. She had never seen anything like this before. She had seen the occasional lost soul walking around, but they were never this defined, and they never gave any sign that they knew she could see them. As Anne walked, she felt dread and the hairs on her skin began to stand up. Against her better judgment, Anne turned to look over her shoulder to see the demon directly behind her, following her. The young woman had never been so terrified and quickened her pace to a slow jog.

When she looked behind again, the demon was even closer as he appeared to glide slightly above the ground. Anne broke into an all-out sprint, running as fast as she could nearly knocking over a group of young men in the process.

"Hey, watch out!" one yelled.

"Crazy ass woman!" exclaimed another.

But there *was* someone after her or to be more specific something. Anne looked back again, hoping the monstrosity had disappeared, but it was still directly behind her following and looking with intense curiosity and wonder.

Tears began to form in Anne's eyes as she ran as fast as she could dashing around people and across a crosswalk nearly getting hit by a car as the driver blared their horn at her yelling obscenities from the window. She ran until she saw what she was hoping to find. A cathedral.

Anne was not a religious person but was often able to find refuge in and around churches. She ran with all her might until she got to the steps. As she turned back to look at the demon, she ran directly into a wall of a man exiting the church.

She almost fell to the ground, but the man caught her.

"Ma'am, are you okay?" he asked, able to clearly see the distress this young woman was in.

Anne looked behind her to see the demon stopped several feet away. It wasn't on holy grounds yet, but it was clearly not wanting to advance any further. Anne watched as the demon looked from her to the man. It appeared both angry and afraid

6

as it snarled and began to turn away, returning to its incorporeal form of dark matter before disappearing entirely.

"Miss," the man said as he tried to see what this woman was so afraid of.

He saw nothing behind her but a few strange looks from passersby.

Anne turned to face the man and immediately saw the bright light emanating from his head with a large light essence just behind him. He was a tall man, well over six-foot, with an athletic build, short brown hair, and facial stubble. She could barely see his deep blue eyes through his light.

Anne stood up and composed herself as she wiped the tears from her eyes.

"I'm fine," she forced a smile then began to move past the man to the cathedral doors.

He was about to ask if he could help her with anything, but she was inside before he could speak.

Anne didn't care for churches or more specifically she didn't care for the people in the churches. She was actually quite fond of the buildings, as they always brought her a sense of peace. She never saw any of the dark entities in churches, but the parishioners themselves sometimes held the darkest light within them. Still, she felt at peace on holy ground. One of Anne's favorite things was when a church had a courtyard or

7

outside garden with statues or a bench. More than once she had spent the night in such places.

No one was at the entrance to see Anne walk past the bowl of Holy Water and forego the usual crossing of oneself as she walked into the hall. The cathedral was large and adorned with beautiful architecture and works of art. It was dimly lit for the afternoon, with just a few bands of light seeping through the stained-glass windows. There were a few people up front praying quietly as Anne sat in the rearmost pew. She didn't bow her head or use the kneeler she simply sat in quiet to regain her calm. She was still shaken by what she had seen, and more specifically that *it* had seen her. Anne deepened her breath when a sliver of sunlight caught her attention as it shone through the stained-glass window closest to her. What she saw was an armored man with wings and a sword that she knew must be an Angel with his foot on the head of something that looked strikingly similar to what was chasing her just moments before.

"Archangel Michael, the leader of Angels. This is one of my favorite depictions of him."

Anne was startled by the priest. She was so entranced by the stained-glass mural, she didn't notice his approach.

"I'm sorry, I didn't mean to scare you," the priest said.

Anne felt uncomfortable and began to get up, but the priest immediately placed his hands out. "Please stay, I'll leave if you like."

Anne hesitated for a moment as she sheepishly eyed the priest. He was dressed in the usual vestments and looked to be in his mid-fifties. His hair was a mix of white and sandy blonde, and he had light skin that bared the weathering of an older man. His light was not as bright as the man Anne ran into outside the cathedral, but it pulsed with a warm glow that made her feel at peace. She slowly returned to her seat and smiled slightly.

The priest smiled. "I have some things I have to do, but do you mind if I join you for a moment?"

Anne really didn't like talking to people, particularly those in a position of authority, but she felt a familiar feeling with this man, something she hadn't felt in a long time. He felt... fatherly. She gave the smallest of nods.

The priest smiled and plopped down on the pew a bit jovially.

"Thank you. I swear on my mother's potato salad, Sister Helen is relentless about designing our flyers for the crawfish boil."

He waived at a nun towards the front of the church who just looked at him oddly.

"I'm Father Daniel."

Not waiting or even giving enough time for a response, Father Daniel just continued talking as if he'd known Anne her whole life.

"Do you know much about Michael?" he asked, looking back up

at the mural.

Anne shook her head no.

Father Daniel nodded slightly. "As I said before, he is considered by many to be the leader of the angels, behind Jesus, of course."

Father Daniel placed one hand on his chin as he studied the window like he'd done probably a thousand times before. Anne looked intently at the mural as well.

"He was sent to Moses, Jacob, and Abraham, but is known primarily as a warrior angel, a protector to all of us."

As Anne's eyes moved from Michael to the demon under his foot, a wave of fear sent a shiver down her spine as she thought of the thing that was chasing her just moments before.

With a small trembling voice, Anne asked, "Who... what is he stepping on?"

Father Daniel could sense Anne's discomfort. Although she didn't see him, Father Daniel had noticed Anne when she entered the cathedral and could clearly see she was suffering. He deeply cared for people, particularly young ones that are lost. As a priest, many would say that his goal is to bring people to Christ, but he would always disagree.

My job is to help people see the good in themselves and others. If I can do that, Jesus will take care of the rest.

"So that image is a replica of the original done by Raphael, the artist, not the ninja turtle."

Anne turned her head for a moment at the baffling priest before he continued. "So, this is his depiction of the battle between Michael and Lucifer."

Anne started visibly shaking as tears came to her eyes. Was the monster that was chasing her actually... the devil?

"But that's not what he looks like," Father Daniel quickly added after seeing Anne's response.

Anne turned to the priest to look at him, more afraid of the thing that had chased her than this stranger seeing her cry. She wiped her tears as he continued.

"At least I don't think he does. No, Lucifer was supposed to be the most beautiful angel. I think the image is a representation of who the devil was, his vile, deceivingly evil soul portrayed externally."

Anne broke down sobbing. This priest could never understand, no one could. She pulled her heels onto the edge of her seat, wrapped her arms around her knees, and cried uncontrollably.

Father Daniel felt her pain. He wanted to hold her, to comfort her, to tell her it would be okay, but he wouldn't cross that line of physical contact. Being a priest, he was especially careful with touching anyone due to the stigma that had permeated the Catholic Church, which was more difficult than he would ever admit. Feeling the warmth of Jesus's embrace, Father Daniel wanted to hug everyone with that same love.

Father Daniel leaned forward and slightly towards Anne. "Is there someone I can call for you? If not, I have a very good friend that works at socia-"

Anne shot up and began backing away down the aisle as she sniffled and tried to control her sobs, "No! I won't talk to anyone! I'm never going back to one of those places *ever again*!"

Father Daniel stood up and put his hands out, signaling Anne to stop, hoping he would get to tell her one more thing. "I won't call anyone, I promise. Please, just one second."

Anne wasn't having it and turned to walk out, but Father Daniel's voice boomed through the church.

"Please!"

Unconcerned with who might be watching or making a scene, Father Daniel just wanted to give a few words that he hoped might help. Anne stopped but did not turn around.

"Please, just one second."

Father Daniel stopped several feet behind Anne.

"I just want you to know you can always call on him, on Michael. Just ask for his protection, but even more than that and I really want you to hear these words. The devil only has as much power as we give him."

Anne turned around enough to make eye contact with Father Daniel, who looked at her with what could only be described as determined love. She nodded slightly, then exited the cathedral.

As soon as the doors closed behind her, Anne stopped as she looked at the light and dark shadows following everyone around. Almost instantly she saw a flash of sparks to her left where the two had collided. She knew she had to compose herself. She walked down the steps and continued her walk down the sidewalk looking back towards the ground trying to avoid all the entities around her.

* * *

The rest of the day went by as smoothly as Anne had hoped. She kept her head down, raising her head only when essential. Eventually, Anne had made her way to one of her favorite places in the city, the Riverwalk. Unlike most tourists, Anne wasn't interested in the host of shops and restaurants that lined the Riverwalk but the space in-between where she could find a bench and listen to the water as the riverboats floated by. Here she found peace in the chaos of the city.

It was after twilight and Anne had decided a couple of hours ago that she would use the bench she was sitting on as a bed tonight. It wasn't the most comfortable, but there was no way she was going to sleep at any of the normal places the homeless people did, not after seeing what she did earlier. She wanted as much privacy as the city would allow, plus the weather was actually nice for once, not too humid.

She still hadn't eaten however, but she did find enough change to add to her $3.48 to get something from the nearby taco stand, maybe some tacos or tamales. She only hoped no one would take her bench before she returned.

Anne began to make her way towards the taco stand. She stopped at a crosswalk and looked up as she waited for the electric sign to change. There was a group of pedestrians waiting to cross so Anne couldn't avoid seeing the light and dark figures all around her. She focused like she had all day on the sign, waiting for the little green walk to appear so she could go back to scanning the ground when a shadow beside her quickly took shape.

Anne couldn't help but look, and to her horror, it was the same monster that had chased her earlier. He studied her intently, almost grinning. Anne was in shock at seeing this creature as she was actively trying not to then as if things couldn't get any worse more shadows started to take form. Demons, every one of them deformed and vile appeared one after another all looking right at her. Frozen in horror, Anne couldn't move even as the crosswalk changed and the group of people began to move on.

The one on her right had skin like a burned snake, and his jaw seemed disjointed and hanging as it oozed some unknown black liquid. In front of her, a large and winged ape-looking creature with blotched burnt fur, large teeth, and a pushed-in nose. Another more feminine one also appeared almost beautiful with long hair and a curvaceous body but her exposed upper body led down to an animal's lower half, full of fur legs complete with

14

hooves. All of them had marks of pain and torture. Scars circled the female demon's wrists, deep burns, lacerations, and tears covered much of the demon's flesh.

But the eyes, their eyes were the most terrifying things about them. Void of all light, they were just shining black orbs that swirled into the depths of an abysmal void.

"Found you!"

Anne slowly turned her head to the demon that had chased her earlier. He stood with his head tilted sideways, still curious as to who this woman was.

"We have someone that would like to meet you," his voice was guttural and slowly paced but unexpectedly articulate.

Anne screamed as she took off, running faster than she ever thought she could. She pushed people out of the way as she looked desperately for a church. She was at least ten blocks from the cathedral, but she knew there was another church nearby, she just didn't know where. She turned down the side of a tall building and cut through the parking garage, not daring to look back. She ran around the back of the building, running right through a drug deal, paying no attention to the armed thugs yelling at her. Anne turned down an alley between two buildings and unexpectantly came to a razor-wire fence that she began to climb.

"Why are you running love?" came a sweet sultry voice.

Anne looked over her shoulder to see the female demon.

"You can't escape us. You might as well embrace us."

The succubus laughed as the lead demon appeared to raise his eyebrows at her.

Anne sliced herself on the razor wire and fell down crying, "No, no, no!"

She fell into the corner of the fence and the building once again, bringing her knees to her chest and tucking her head down. She could feel them standing around her.

The lead demon spoke again in his unnatural voice. "There is nothing to be afraid of."

A few disgusting laughs like guttural hyenas could be heard.

"Okay, there is plenty to be afraid of. Ha-ha-ha!" the demon's laughs continued loudly.

If the arrogant demons had listened for a moment, they might have felt fear as the young women they tormented whispered to herself because in her whispers was a name, a name they were deathly afraid of.

"Archangel Michael, please protect me! Archangel Michael, please protect me! Archangel Michael, please protect me!" Anne spoke through the tears, she spoke with all of her heart, with all of her faith she called for help.

The laughing stopped as a bright light formed in the alley. Anne lifted her head, her eyes squinting from the light. She had seen the light beings before, but they had never taken shape. Anne watched in awe as the figure of a winged man appeared.

An angel, but not like the one in the stained-glass picture. This one was perfect, at least he was the most perfect thing that Anne had ever seen. He looked like a man of average size, wearing a flowing white tunic with green and gold trim and bare feet. He had perfectly dark tanned skin that seemed as smooth as marble, his thick dark brown hair was short but seemed to flow through the air as if in a breeze and he had large translucent wings that seemed to glisten a pearl color.

Through all the beauty in this creature, Anne was most captivated by two things. His eyes were a beautiful brown but seemed to glisten in the light around him, drawing Anne's attention to them. But the thing that captivated Anne the most was the feeling she felt that emanated from him. The strongest feeling Anne had ever felt, and it was good, pure... it was love. The angel exuded love from every essence of his being, yet as much as he projected love. He was visibly angry.

The light behind the Angel dissipated as his feet hit the ground. He never looked at Anne but eyed the demons as he stood protecting her.

"Ahhhh!" the lead demon hissed. "You can't keep all of us from her!"

The angel lifted his head and spoke in an old, middle eastern accent. "What is your name, demon?"

The group of demons groaned as they knew the power of giving over their name. The angel gave a slight chuckle to goad the arrogant demons.

The demon that first chased Anne was the only one brave enough to speak up. "My name is Alyas, which means despair in the common tongue, and I do not fear you, slave!"

The angel stood tall.

"Thank you. This one is my charge, and no harm will come to her."

The angel turned his right hand open and as he did, a curved scimitar sword of gold light slowly materialized in it.

"You do not need to fear me, demon, but the name Abdiel was gifted to me by my father. That, Alyas, servant of lies, you *will* fear."

The angel Abdiel's pearlescent wings pushed down as he jumped high into the air towards the demons. The satanic spawn hurried to move out of the way as each began materializing their own weapons of darkness. Alyas quickly moved behind the large, winged ape-like demon, kicking him in the small of his back towards the angel.

The large demon was in the middle of bringing forth a weapon, but Abdiel sliced clean through the creature from its right shoulder to its left hip before it had a chance. The demon screamed in agony before disintegrating to ash and returning to the abyss.

Abdiel was surprised by an ethereal black axe that swung down at his head through the disappearing ashes but was able to get his sword up in time to block Alyas's blow leading to spectacular sparks as the weapons clashed. To his right, the snake-skinned demon launched at him with a gruesome spear with a pole that seemed to mimic his slimy skin. Abdiel quickly pushed Alyas's blocked ax up and kicked him back just in time to parry the spear's attack, sending the snake-skinned demon falling past.

Abdiel then raised his weapon over his head to strike down on Alyas, but as he did, the succubus' blood-red whip wrapped around his wrist. The dark whip burned on the angel's wrist, sending electric pain through his arm. Abdiel pulled the whip taught as his sword dematerialized from his right hand and re-materialized in his left. He then turned and cut down, severing the whip from his arm, making an incredible firework-like display upon impact, sending the succubus back a few steps.

The Angel could sense Alyas behind him and could see the snake skinned demon approaching again with his spear. He pushed his wings down as he launched himself into the air, backflipping over Alyas until he had all of the demons in view. He stayed in the air as his scimitar disappeared and he began flinging shards of light daggers at his foes.

The snake-skinned demon screamed as one hit his neck before he could generate an ethereal shield like the other two did. He stumbled to the ground but materialized a dark, massive shield before getting hit again.

Abdiel continued his relentless assault of light shards creating a beautiful light display as each one met a demon's shield until he suddenly shot up out of sight for an instant before coming down like a missile with his own spear of divine light to impale the snake skinned demon to the ground.

Abdiel removed his spear from the howling demon, sending him back to hell. As the ashes blew away Abdiel stood staring at Alyas and the succubus who were now both full of fear.

Anne laid in the corner in awe at what she was seeing as she thought to herself aloud, "Every time... Is this what is happening?"

Anne had seen the sparks since she was a child. She knew that they always meant that light and dark were touching but she never imagined it was a battle.

"Beautiful, isn't it?"

Anne was startled by a voice coming behind her on the other side of the fence. She leaned away to look at what she could only describe as a well-dressed being. His skin was a light olive and, like the angel, appeared flawless. His hair was black, and he wore an all-black suit complete with a black shirt and tie. Anne had noticed that the eyes of these beings told the most about who they were, and while this one's eyes were a dark brown, they looked rather human. Anne thought how easy it would be for this one to blend in with every other human but for one glaring thing, this being had no light. No dark or bright light exuded from his head like every person she had ever seen. That and the fact that he was commenting on something she thought only she could see was what told her he was not of our world.

As he looked at her, Anne's fear began to rise, as if sensing this the man spoke.

"Do not be afraid, I am not going to harm you."

His voice was calm and soothing as he spoke with an accent that sounded almost Latin but from no specific country. He smiled and Anne was entranced by him as he continued.

"You can see them?" the man pointed with his eyes towards the battle.

Anne turned momentarily to see the angel slam the female demon into the side of the building so hard she swore she saw the bricks move in from the force as the demon fell away into nothingness.

She looked back at the man. "Yes, I... I've always seen them. I mean not like this, but..."

"Come with me, I want to show you something," the man calmly said as if they were old friends.

Anne looked perplexed but was drawn to this man for some reason. He didn't say anything else, but pointed to the lowest part of the fence pole nearest to her. Anne could see the piece of metal banding meant to hold the fence to the post was gone, all she had to do was lift up the fence and roll under it. She didn't know why she didn't see that before, but it was there, a way out of this alley. She looked back at the man, who smiled slightly.

"I promise, I won't hurt you and I can keep them away from you."

Without thinking, Anne slowly began to get up and move toward the gate.

"Ahhhh! I'll find you!"

Anne fell back down to the ground at the curses Alyas leveled at Abdiel as the angel removed his sword from the demon's chest. Immediately, Abdiel looked past Anne and locked eyes with the mysterious man.

"Begone from this one, Azazel, or I will send you back to your master as I did your siblings."

Again, the angel seemed to ignore Anne as she looked from him to the man in the suit. The man's eyes seemed to get darker as his eyes narrowed.

"If you know who I am, pawn, then you know I am no lesser demon," Azazel sneered at Abdiel.

Abdiel walked closer, his scimitar in hand. "I am named Abd-"

Azazel forcefully spoke up. "I don't care what your name is, pawn. You are nothing but a lower animal, unfit to have wings. I may not be able to kill you, but I can inflict pain upon you so great that you will fall to your knees in the service of my master, begging for reprieve."

Azazel's eyes slowly became black as he spewed his vile words through an evil grimace.

"Just as so many of your kind have done."

Azazel's voice then returned to its calm, enchanting tone as he returned his gaze to Anne. "Now, leave us pawn, while you can."

Abdiel calmly walked forward until he was standing directly in front of Anne. He dematerialized his sword and folded his arms as he stood looking at Azazel through the fence who returned his gaze to the angel, anger stirring in his eyes.

Darkness began to form around Azazel and his body appeared to grow. His pupils were becoming darker and darker as hatred filled his body.

"Have it your way pawn, you wi-"

Abdiel smiled slightly as he cut Azazel off. "Have you met my brother, Michael?"

Immediately Azazel began to shrink back to his former human-like form, infuriated and angry.

Abdiel nodded a bit. "I believe you have met him. It's been a while though, right? Perhaps I should call on him."

Azazel's body shook with fury as he growled low under his breath before disappearing in a dark cloud.

Abdiel let out a visible sigh, obviously thankful that he left.

"So, you're not Michael, then?" Anne asked in a soft but clear voice.

Abdiel looked at Anne, who was looking straight at him, talking to him. Now, the angel truly did have an expression of fear as he realized that she could see and hear him.

Angels by nature were pure and didn't throw curses, but there was a word they used as an expletory in times of extreme surprise or uncertainty.

Abdiel's beautiful brown eyes grew wide, "Charit!"

He then disappeared into a cloud of light.

Chapter 2: The Lamb and the bull

There are rules to the universe, created and implemented by God. Some of these rules are of a nature such as gravity, time, and space but those rules only exist to supplement the greatest gift God gives to all of his creations, free will. No being created by the father is created without this gift, to include humans, angels, and even the Lamb himself. One rule is that while the material world and the spirit world exist simultaneously, those from the material world are not supposed to see the spiritual world. This is because of the effect seeing such a thing would have over a person's free will in their life on earth and how that may affect God's plans for them. God, in his infinite wisdom, has plans for all of us, even the Angels and the Lamb. But it is our free will to choose to walk the path laid out for us, or stray from it. Only the Lamb was to know of his path. God does not like to see his children suffer, but without trials, there can be no rejoicing and no victory. The Lamb *chose* to walk his path not because he was meant to, but because he loves us. He chose to suffer for us.

We are all made of our Father in his image, and sometimes that part of us glimpses the spiritual world. Others have opened doorways to commune with lost spirits and demons. But none has ever been able to see and hear the spiritual world like Anne, and according to the rules of the universe, none should. That is why Abdiel was so shocked when Anne spoke to him. She has broken through the veil and in doing so has broken one of God's laws.

Abdiel needed guidance, so he went to the greatest source of guidance the universe has ever known.

Moving through time and space was instant for an angel. All they need to do is think of where they want to go, and they arrive in the blink of an eye. They can also find and teleport to beings that retain the part of them that is of God. This works more like a beacon and is more complex. Essentially, the more light a being has in them, the easier they are to locate and the power to sense the light and dark of a being, be it angel, human, or demon, is within everyone to one degree or another. It was easy for Abdiel to find Jesus, as his light shone brightest of all.

In a split second, the angel appeared in a room with a dozen ramshackle beds filled with children. Even more, littered the ground of the room on cheap bedrolls. Since Abdiel teleported to a person, it took him a moment to realize the location. A makeshift hospital on the outskirts of Kolkata India for sick children.

Angels carried deep empathy for humans, and so Abdiel's urgency and excitement were immediately brought down to a mix of deep sadness and peace. As he looked around Abdiel saw many young ones, he knew would be leaving the material world soon and many more who suffered from debilitating illnesses that they probably wouldn't recover from. Close to each child stood a guardian angel ready to embrace the young children as they passed over into an existence of no pain, no suffering, and pure love.

Typically, when a human is near death a guardian needs to remain vigilant, ever ready to ward off demons that may try to spew their vile corruption and feed off the dark energy of a bitter soul but usually, by that point, the human has already made their choice to walk with the light or fall with the darkness. The guardians of these children didn't have to worry about that however, as no demon or fallen angel would dare come to this place, not while the Lamb was here.

Abdiel looked at the children in pain and the tireless workers trying to comfort them. He looked a few beds over past his fellow guardian angels to see Jesus sitting on the side of a little one's bed.

He was a stark contrast to the perfect angels that filled the room as he kept his human form. He was dressed in robes of white with tan and brown trim that extended past his feet. His skin was light brown, touched by the sun. He retained his wrinkles and blemishes and as he laid his hand on the child's chest, his wrist bared one of his many scars. His brown hair was clean and wavy, but also looked somewhat messy and unkempt. His cheeks held deep lines from smiling that even his beard couldn't hide. His nose was slightly larger than average, something he often joked came from his mother's side.

There is light and darkness behind every being's eyes and

angels are known to have the most beautiful eye's but there is something far more behind the eyes of the Lamb. They didn't shine like an angel's as they were human eyes, but in them, there was so much more than color. If one was to look into Jesus's eyes to decipher their color, the only answer you could come up with is love. A look from the Son can move the mightiest of warriors or the highest of angels to tears of joy.

Abdiel knew what was happening and didn't want to interrupt. The child Jesus sat with was a little boy of six who was filled with tubes and hooked up to one of the few available monitors. His breath was shallow, and his heartbeat grew weaker with each breath. His mother kneeled next to the bed, holding his hand, crying low sobs. His father stood next to her with his hand on her shoulder, hating himself for not achieving more, thinking maybe if he would have worked harder, he could have afforded better health care. He held in as much pain as he could, trying to be strong for his wife and dying son.

Behind both of them were their own guardians who felt so deeply their pain and behind Jesus smiling slightly was a beautiful dark-haired female angel. She was the boy's guardian and looked forward to the end of his suffering and being his escort on the way home.

Close to death, the boy awoke and was able to see Jesus and his guardian angel on his left side. The love he felt was unlike anything he'd ever felt before, and it gave him just enough strength to turn his head to his parents and smile.

Though he couldn't speak, his eyes told his parents how much he loved them, and they would cherish that last smile every day until they met again.

The boy let out his last breath and slowly looked around.

He looked up to Jesus, who smiled at him. "Hello Nitesh, it is so good to meet you."

Nitesh sat up with vigor and instantly wrapped his arms around Jesus, who embraced him.

"I, I am healed, I... feel better!" Nitesh exclaimed as he buried his head in the chest of the Lamb.

The boy sat back from Jesus and looked at his parents, who were both crying over his empty body. He knew that he had died. He knew that it was coming as he began to see glimmers of light around the room minutes before. As overjoyed as he was to be with Jesus, he was sad for his parents.

Jesus felt Nitesh's sadness deeply. "They are going to be okay," he said calmly.

Nitesh looked at him and smiled, feeling the certainty in his words.

"Your father is a good man. With your mother's help, he will bring healers and medicine to this place. In their love for you, your parents will save many children," Jesus smiled widely. "And you know you will see them again."

29

He winked at Nitesh, who smiled back.

After a moment, Nitesh's eyes got big, "Wait! Is my Nani here?"

Jesus turned to the beautiful dark-haired angel behind him. "This is Batya. She has bee-"

Nitesh excitedly interrupted. "I know you. I think... I've seen you."

Jesus looked to Batya, who was smiling widely with her hand out. "Come on, your Nani is waiting and is very excited."

Nitesh hopped up and took Batya's hand but let go and turned around to Jesus, who was standing behind him.

He wrapped his arms around Jesus's waist, then looked up to him. "Please stay with them for a little while."

Jesus looked at Nitesh, moved by his purity and love. He knelt down to eye level.

"That is why I am here," he then patted Nitesh's shoulder. "Go see your Nani. I will see you later."

Nitesh smiled, then grabbed Batya's hand as they disappeared into a portal of white light.

As urgent as Abdiel's situation was, he couldn't help but smile at the interaction. For humans, death is a sad time, a time for loss, a time for grieving but for guardian angels of those who have walked with the light it was a time of joy. Every human has an angel assigned to them at birth to watch over and guide them on the path God has laid out for them. Every day without wavering, the angels fight for their humans against evil. They grow very close to their wards, feeling their happiness and sadness. The reward for a guardian is when their human finally gets to meet them, gets to embrace them, and when they get to escort them home to Father. Guardian angels cherish this moment every time and seeing it, even when it was not his ward, still brought joy to Abdiel.

"Abdiel, I have not seen you in some time," Jesus exclaimed with his arms open wide.

Abdiel was an angel, pure in heart, with great power, and is known as a warrior among other angels, but none of that mattered in the presence of Jesus. He moved quickly to embrace him, much as Nitesh did for the first time.

After a few moments, Abdiel pulled back, his urgency and fear returning. "Lord, I have encountered something with my ward that..."

The guardian struggled to find the words.

"I need your counsel, Lord."

Jesus turned, "And you shall have it, brother."

He turned to look at the morning parents still crying over their son's passing. Jesus felt all of their pain, and all of their suffering as tears began to form in his loving eyes.

He lifted his head to compose himself. "Walk with me, they need some time."

Jesus looked at the couple's guardian angels who were draped over the defeated parents crying with them.

As Abdiel began to follow Jesus, he thought maybe he needed some time too, his compassion never ceasing the Lamb truly felt the parents' pain.

Jesus made his way out of the building as Abdiel followed. "Tell me, what has got you so concerned?"

Abdiel took a breath. "The girl I have been assigned was attacked by demons. At first, I just thought it was strange as there were those of lust, greed, and wrath there. I've never sensed such things in her but..."

"But that hasn't stopped them from trying before," Jesus said as he shook his head, anger rising.

"Exactly," Abdiel agreed. "My ward, she has a connection to our world stronger than any I have ever seen."

Jesus's eyebrows raised. "Did she seek this connection?"

The simple question had much more behind it. Abdiel knew that what Jesus meant was had Anne been trying to commune with the spirit world through divination or tools of witchcraft.

Abdiel shook his head as the two continued down a wooded path behind the hospital. "No, my Lord, not at all. This is a gift she has had since she arrived, I presume it was given to her by Father, but I do not know the purpose."

Jesus nodded, as it was not all that unusual for God to gift certain humans in this way.

"I knew she could see beyond her world but..." Abdiel stopped and turned directly to Jesus, "She can see our world... clearly."

Jesus's eyebrows raised. "What do you mean?"

Abdiel took a breath. "Lord, she can see our world as we do but more than that..." the guardian shook his head still not believing what had transpired. "She can hear and understand us."

Very few things brought surprise to Jesus, but this revelation most certainly did. "Are you sure?"

Before Abdiel had a chance to respond Jesus had waved off the question as he thought for a moment.

"How old is this girl?" Jesus asked.

Abdiel answered, "She has spent nearly twenty cycles on earth."

Again, Jesus was surprised as he raised an eyebrow. "She is a young woman. You did not know she had this gift before?"

Abdiel shook his head. "No, Lord. I've always known she

could see more, but I believe her abilities have recently become stronger. She has always been lukewarm and so my connection to her was never very strong."

Jesus knew that what Abdiel was referring to was her light. Most humans are referred to as lukewarm, tepid, or somewhat good. They arrive in the material world with the light of the Father shining bright, but for the majority, that light is dimmed over time until it becomes only a small steady glow.

Jesus stopped for a moment as he looked down in thought, trying to understand this young woman's purpose.

"There is something else," Abdiel said as Jesus returned his gaze to him. "Azazel was there too."

Jesus's face of surprise and curiosity turned to concern. "You fought him?"

Abdiel shook his head. "Thankfully, I didn't have to," the Angel smiled a bit. "I did ask if he wanted to see Michael and offered to call on him, but he... declined."

Jesus laughed. "He does have that effect on them, doesn't he!" He walked closer and put a hand on Abdiel's shoulder. "I am proud of you."

If angels had a weakness, it was their pride. They knew the Father and in knowing him had unwavering courage and confidence, but far too many angels had fallen thinking their power was theirs and not Gods. Azazel was one of those angels whose pride and arrogance led him to fall. He became the chief general in the army of the great deceiver and brought great wickedness upon the earth until Father sent Michael, who cast him down to join his master in the pits of hell.

Abdiel would have sacrificed himself to save Anne, such was the love of angels, but he knew how great a foe Azazel was as he was fallen from the highest order of angels. He was thankful that he didn't have to fight him.

"Give me a moment, Abdiel," Jesus said, to which Abdiel nodded.

Jesus moved several feet away, clasped his hands together, and began to whisper in prayer as he communed with Father, trying to understand his will. Abdiel too closed his eyes and dipped his head in prayer.

It wasn't long before the Angel heard Jesus softly speak, "Thank you, Father." He turned and walked back to Abdiel. Jesus let out a small breath. "He won't tell me much."

Those words spoke volumes to both Abdiel and Jesus, alluding to a grander plan that even the Lamb was a part of.

Jesus nodded slightly. "This woman, her path is very important. I do not know why yet, but it will be revealed soon." The Lamb looked directly at Abdiel, emphasizing his next words, "She is in danger, from both worlds."

These words sent shivers down Abdiel's spine that reached to the tips of his folded wings. He could protect Anne from demons,

35

but held little power in the material world. He looked down, concerned as Jesus continued.

"The enemy wants her, I do not know why, but they are already communing with Lucifer's followers in the material world. There is a man you must take her to, she has already crossed paths with this man and his guardian is keeping him in place waiting for your arrival."

Abdiel was curious. Who was this man that walked so much in the light as to be so easily guided. Furthermore, who was his guardian?

Sensing the Angel's curiosity, Jesus answered the question before Abdiel asked, "The man's name.... well, he goes by a few different ones, but Rahim is his guardian."

Abdiel's eyes grew wide. There were billions of guardian angels, but there were less than fifty twiceborn angels. A twiceborn angel is an angel who was born a human, but through their great service on earth were born into angels by Father upon their human death. The two most commonly used examples of this are the Prophets Elijah and Enoch who became the Archangels Sandalphon and Metatron.

Abdiel had never met Rahim, but his feats and devotion to Father were known long before he became a twiceborn angel.

"This man, Father, must have great plans to give him such a guardian," Abdiel said.

Jesus nodded. "Indeed, and you must go now. The time is short."

Abdiel was stunned but hadn't received the guidance he came for.

"But Lord, what shall I do? If this woman can see and understand us... how am I to follow Father's law? What do I... what can I say that won't alter her path? I don't understand."

All Angels strictly obeyed God's laws and the chief among them was to not directly alter the path of a human's free will. An angel's primary task was guidance, not direction. On occasion when a human hears a voice that drastically alters their course or even more so is physically moved to safety to avoid bodily harm or death, that can be in direction from Father but more than likely that guardian angel is acting of his own will. Guardians grow attached to their humans and love them deeply. Sometimes that attachment causes them to influence their ward's free will, which carries the worst punishment a guardian can receive, to be taken away from the one they've cared for since birth and given stewardship over another. This is heartbreaking to a guardian which is why Abdiel carried such fear.

Jesus smiled at Abdiel. An Angel created by God full of love and still humble and insecure.

"Abdiel, my brother, Father picked Rahim to be the guardian of this man," he placed a hand on the Angel's shoulder, "and he chose you, Abdiel, to be Anne's guardian. Trust in yourself as

37

you trust in him and reveal what your heart tells you to."

Slowly, Abdiel nodded. He was still fearful but just as he was meant to guide Anne on her path, clearly, she too, was a part of his.

* * *

The room was dark, lit by just a few candles, the majority of which set upon an altar made of stone. A statue of a man with a bull's head was the figurehead of the alter, his arms raised with palms outward. In front of the statue was a large oval basin about four feet in length that had char and ash on the bottom. Around the basin were stone carvings of the same bull-headed figure along with demons, fire, and screaming children.

On his knees in front of the altar was a man of average build and subhuman morality. His cropped graying brown hair made him look considerably older than the thirty years he was. He wore jeans and a tucked-in Polo shirt that didn't seem to go with the demonic symbols and inverted pentagram that covered the floor around him.

Sebastian wasn't particularly educated, and he didn't come from a family of influence. He rarely spoke of his upbringing, saying it was a trite story of a drunk father, whore mother and that he ran away at 16. It was unusual for someone of such low social standing to be accepted into his order, but Sebastian had a talent that caught the attention of the ascended masters. He had a talent for communicating with the other side.

What Sebastian had was not a gift, but knowledge. Knowledge passed down through the ages easily researched and studied. The ability to commune with the other side was reckless and almost always brought pain and suffering, but that could be postponed if a person was willing to submit to whatever reached out from the void, then the reward would be information and information meant power. It was never a being of light that answered the call. Occasionally it was a lost soul, trapped in between worlds unable to move on but more often than not if you try to reach out to the other side it will be demons who responded. Demons fed off the energy of chaos, fear, anger, and destruction and were happy to torment any human they could, but nothing brought a demon more pleasure than to use a human to inflict even more pain on the world of man.

Sebastian was silent in his dark prayers as he called out for the knowledge that would elevate his status. He slowly rocked back and forth waiting for an image to appear in the black void of his mind when he heard one word vilely whispered in his ear, "*Name.*"

Sebastian's green eyes shot open as he quickly rose to his feet and moved to an old wooden table off to the side of the room. He sat down in the chair and pulled up, looking upon the alphabet board before him. Similar to a ouija board the top half of the alphabet board had every letter listed in a semicircle from a to z while the lower half held six slots with different symbols each correlating to a specific task. Sebastian opened a small wooden box from in front of the chart and withdrew a black velvet bag. He withdrew from the bag a long chain with a brass weight on the end.

Sebastian stilled himself as he held the pendulum over the center of the board. "In the name of Baal devourer of mankind, I submit myself as your mouthpiece. Use me as you see fit and I will sacrifice in your name!"

The pendulum hung perfectly still as Sebastian repeated the chant.

Slowly the pendulum began to move, picking up momentum backward and forward until it was a steady swing.

"What name?" Sebastian asked.

Slowly the pendulum changed direction until it swung directly towards a letter.

"A," the evil man said, confirming the letter before the pendulum moved to the next letter.

"N," again confirming the letter, Sebastian watched as the pendulum swirled in a circle before returning to the same letter.

"N"

The pendulum again changed direction as it moved to the final letter.

"E," Sabastian said as the pendulum returned to a very slow but steady circle.

"Anne is the name?" the man asked as the pendulum swung

back and forth, telling him yes. "Am I to find this girl?"

Again, the pendulum swung forward and back.

"What is her last name?"

The pendulum swung in a circle again, signifying that the demon communicating did not know.

"Where is she?" Sebastian asked, needing more information. The demon gave a word, *here*.

Sebastian knew the demon meant here in the city, but New Orleans was a big city, and he would need much more information before he could start his task. Through the same long process of communication, Sebastian was able to write a list of words the demon communicated.

- *Anne*
- *New Orleans*
- *Poydras street*
- *Red Hair*
- *Young*

Not a lot of information, but enough to begin his task. Sebastian only had one more question for the demon.

"What am I to do with her?"

The pendulum began to sway widely towards one of the bottom sections of the board. It swung so high that the weight would drop as it lost momentum at the top of its swing. Sebastian knew that the entity wanted to make its point clear on this matter as he looked to the instructions in that area that simply said, "Capture."

Sebastian quickly got up from the table and made his way from the basement into the storage room of the lodge. He closed the shelf door behind him hiding the entrance and immediately made his way to the ascended master's office.

As he walked in, he noticed the lodge master having coffee with the Sheriff.

Sebastian nodded slightly. "Please, excuse my interruption."

Sheriff Landry waved Sebastian in. "Nonsense, brother. Come join us. Our esteemed lodge master, and I were just reminiscing about that time we broke into the supposed crypt of that voodoo queen."

The lodge master laughed at the memory as he spoke in a thick Cajun accent, adding to Sheriff Landry's story. "As I recall, you damn near soiled your britches when you saw dat snake."

The Sheriff lifted an eyebrow. "I know you put that snake there, T-Bro!"

Laney Broussard was a powerful man who had connections all over the city, not the least of which was Sheriff Landry, who was a high member of their lodge.

Laney sat back in his chair and laughed as it creaked. "Maybe I did, maybe I didn't."

Sebastian stood with one arm at the waist, with the elbow of his other resting in his palm. His feet were at a forty-five-degree angle and he tugged his earlobe slightly. To an outsider, this might look like an awkward way to stand, but to an initiate of the mystery schools, this sent a message.

Laney Broussard saw Sebastian's stance and knew immediately that whatever he had come for was important. "What is it Sebastian, is there something you need to tell me?"

Sebastian looked to the Sheriff who understood the situation. "I see you two have important business with *the work.* I'll leave y'all to it."

Landry got up and moved to the door.

"Give me a holler later there, T-Bro," the Sheriff turned and winked. "We'll have to go check out dat voodoo queen's grave again."

Laney laughed, "Okay Landry, you take care now."

When the door shut behind them, the lodge master's demeanor changed. "What is it?"

Sebastian respected the Ascended Master but knew that his

information came from a source with more authority, Laney knew this too as the young initiate spoke.

"I have received a direct message, sir. It was quite strong and explicit."

Laney sat forward, wondering what orders came from their dark master.

"We are to find a girl and capture her. I do not know the purpose yet but..."

Broussard's eyes narrowed. "But what?"

Sebastian stepped forward a bit. "Sir, this is the strongest message I've ever received. I don't know who this girl is but our master wants her badly."

Laney thought for a moment as he rubbed his white-whiskered chin. "Okay, do you know where she is?"

Sebastian nodded. "As of ten minutes ago, I was told she was on Poydras."

This made Laney's eyes wide. It was rare to receive such direct information.

"Okay, call Junior and Tripp, they can help you find her."

The lodge master looked off for a moment.

"I'll prepare our holding area but if you have to, bring her to Father Peters, he has an alter room that has chains. I'll call him just in case."

Sebastian nodded and turned to begin his task.

"Sebastian!" Laney called.

"Yes, sir?" the initiate answered.

"This is of importance to our master, it could be what elevates our lodge to... more networking opportunities," Laney said in a hopeful voice.

Sebastian nodded again. "My thoughts as well, master. We will bring the girl back."

What the ascended master of the lodge meant when he said "networking opportunities" was that his lodge could be given the resources to house more children in their works for child trafficking. More children meant more money for the lodge, more pleasure, and more sacrifices in the name of their master, Baal.

Chapter 3: The Guided

Anne's fear was overwhelmed by her developed senses. Ever since her experience in the alley, there were no more wisps of light and dark. Anne clearly saw angels and demons. She had walked for most of the night trying her best to stay around restaurants and nighttime shopping areas as they held a greater abundance of angels, where the back alleys and dimly lit neighborhoods held demons around every corner.

She quickly realized that they didn't know she could see them, so if she acted relatively normal and didn't look directly at one for too long, she could slip by unnoticed. What really gave Anne the confidence to walk by was that her prayers worked. She had never really prayed before, not like that. Of course, she had never been so terrified in all her life, so she assumed that had something to do with it, but regardless, it worked. She kept thinking to herself all night. *I prayed for help and an angel, a real angel came!*

"And he kicked ass too!" Anne muttered to herself, a bit louder than she meant to.

She sat on a bench watching the flow of cars and people begin their early morning commutes. She could see now that whenever an Angel touched the head of a human, a glow would momentarily appear. She watched this happen multiple times, and she was beginning to see a pattern. Once a woman was about to get on the bus when an angel touched her head and she suddenly turned around to find her phone had fallen on the ground. She watched another angel touch a man's head as he was about to walk across an intersection, and he stopped just for a moment to check his watch as a car flew by running a stop sign clearly keeping him from getting hit. But her favorite observance was a woman who was leaving a restaurant and just as she was about to turn towards her car an angel touched her head and she dropped her keys. At that same moment, a man was walking from around the building looking down on his phone when his Angel touched his head and he looked up to see the woman that dropped her keys.

Anne didn't know what they were saying, but it looked as if they knew each other and hadn't seen each other for a long time. They talked for almost an hour as Anne watched both their lights grow brighter together. She wondered, was this a chance encounter?

The demons too had a similar effect as they seemed to whisper next to a person's ear. This was particularly clear as people bumped into each other and yelled obscenities or as a parent talked down to their child and also as people were driving. Anne had never realized how many demons there were riding next to drivers feeding into their frustration and anger.

As the warm sun hit her face Anne realized she wasn't scared anymore. For the first time in as long as she could remember she wasn't afraid. Then another thought crossed her mind. Was that angel who protected her, *her* angel? And if so, where was he now?

Anne walked down the street as she tried to remember his name. "Adzel... no... Abeel... no that's not right either... What was it?"

"Abdiel," a voice said as she looked to see the angel that saved her standing casually by her side.

Anne's eyes got wide as she seemed to bounce in excitement, "You! You, you're here!"

Abdiel looked around awkwardly and unsure of himself. He had never directly spoken with someone on the material plane, at least not anyone that could talk back. His beautiful brown eyes darted around under thick eyebrows. His mannerisms were almost childlike, far from the confident warrior Anne remembered. His wings were gone, and he appeared more human.

"I... uh..." Abdiel stuttered.

"What happened to your wings? They didn't fall off or something, right? Did you lose them? Oh my God, I have so many questions. Oh, probably shouldn't have said that, huh? That's a sin, right? I'm a sinner. Oh God, I'm rambling, but you're here! You're really here!"

Abdiel's eyes got bigger as passersby were taking notice of the crazy lady talking to herself, "Perhaps we should find a..." the angel looked around, "more private place to talk."

Slowly Anne became aware of the looks she was getting and tried her best to contain her excitement. She nodded and quickly moved to a nearby alley. There was a wooden fence on the side of the building surrounded by two dumpsters. Anne quickly moved behind them, barely noticing the smell, and turned to Abdiel.

She looked at the Angel in awe, slowly walking around him, looking carefully at his wingless back. There was no mistaking he had them when she first saw him.

Abdiel answered Anne's curiosity by materializing his wings instantly. She stepped back, surprised at their sudden appearance but then moved closer to inspect them. They were absolutely beautiful, pearlescent feathered wings that seemed to vibrate with light. She moved a hand to touch one, but they disappeared as Abdiel turned around to face her.

His unusual accent was calming as he spoke. "You cannot touch my world," As soon as the words exited his mouth Abdiel thought to himself, *well you're not supposed to see it either.*

He then held his hand out, palm open for Anne to touch. She slowly reached her hand out and just when they would have made contact Anne felt a tingle as her hand went through his. Abdiel breathed a sigh of relief. Anne looked at him in wonder, looking behind him for his wings.

"They are there, but we can choose whether to show them or not."

Anne shook her head. "Why would you not show them? They are so beautiful, you are beautiful! I've never seen anything more beautiful than you."

If Abdiel could blush, he most certainly would have. "Thank you, whatever beauty I have was a gift from Father, as were the wings. They are, very special to us."

Anne shook her head as she tried to compartmentalize all the questions racing through her head, but first, she had to tell Abdiel what she'd wanted to say to him all night.

"Thank you! You fought off those things for me. No one's ever stood up for me like that."

She looked down a bit, her insecurity returning.

"Well, you are wrong about that," Abdiel said firmly.

Anne looked up to him as he continued, "I and many others have fought for you before, but there is something you should know. It is a great truth that few humans ever realize."

Whatever nervousness Abdiel had, left him as he stepped closer to Anne.

He leaned in almost to a whisper, "They only have as much power as you give them."

Abdiel stood back up as Anne pondered the thought.

She shook her head. "No, I didn't give them any power. They found me, chased me, and tried to kill me!"

Abdiel shook his head as well. "Did they?" Anne looked confused as the Angel continued, "They can speak to you, follow you, they can influence you, feed off your fear, sadness, and anger *if* you let them, but they cannot touch that which is of the Father unless you willingly submit to them."

Anne tried to make sense of Abdiel's words as she looked down. The Angel moved close again, bending down just enough to make eye contact. "We are his children and are made in his image. As long as we carry his light, they cannot harm us."

Anne raised her head, contemplating the Angel's words.

"The same goes for us," Abdiel said. Anne picked her head up in a look of confusion as he explained. "Above all gifts Father gives, free will is the most sacred. We can guide you, subtly suggest a course that helps you to walk in the light, but we are explicitly forbidden from interfering with your decisions and direction. You called for aid, *that* is why I had the strength to defeat them because *you* gave it to me."

Anne let these words linger for a moment before asking the angel another question she had been wondering. "Speaking of that, I am thankful you came but... I didn't know you. I asked for Michael, he was the only one I thought to ask for help."

Abdiel nodded. "I am your guardian and have been since your arrival here. While time is different in our world, we are bound by the laws of yours and so each of us can only be in one place at any given moment. Michael was helping another, several others actually. When a being prays and they ask Father for help or guidance, when they call on Jesus, it is more often than not an angel who will come on their behalf but in the spirit world, names have power."

Anne shook her head. "I don't understand."

Abdiel paused for a moment to think on how to best explain the power of names. "So, if someone was to call on Jesus and an angel were to arrive in his stead, the Lord's strength and love would enhance that angel's power."

"And so, when I called on Michael..." Anne was putting it together.

"His strength supplemented my own as he is the chief archangel and defender of humanity," Abdiel said, smiling at the thought of his brother.

Michael the valiant warrior sent shivers down the spine of Lucifer's followers, but his love and laughter were even brighter. His fellow Angel's referred to him affectionately as the laughing Angel, unless he was facing a demon, then he embodied all of Father's old anger.

Abdiel smiled widely. "Now, just imagine when you call on Father."

Anne's eyes widened at the thought, then she asked, "You've been with me my whole life?"

The guardian angel's whole being seemed to light up. "Yes, since the beginning. You were easy to guide when you were younger, but as you aged, the demons fed off your fear, and our connection was weakened until you prayed."

Just as Anne was about to speak, Abdiel interrupted, "I am thoroughly enjoying our conversation as it is one I have never had before, but we must move from here. There is someone you need to meet."

Anne shook her head nervously. "Jesus? No, I..." she began to dust off her dirty clothes. "I can't... I am not..."

Anne was insecure and ashamed. Of course, she knew of Jesus but she didn't know anything about him, not really, and she was embarrassed for who she was, for not being a better person.

Abdiel interrupted her nervous ramblings, sad that she felt unworthy of meeting the Lamb when there was no one Jesus felt unworthy of him.

"No, but it is Jesus who told me of him. He is someone from your world. A man who I believe you ran into already."

Anne stopped, perplexed at who this man was and why she had to see him. "I haven't met anyone recently, except for a priest. He was a nice man. Is that who you're talking about?"

Abdiel shook his head. "No, you see the light in them, right?"

He motioned his head towards the sidewalk where the endless flow of people continued to and frow.

Anne nodded. "And the darkness."

The guardian nodded. "Well, is there anyone you've bumped into that had a particularly bright light?"

Anne thought as she considered the question. "The priest had a pretty bright light. I remember a couple with... oh! The man in front of the church! I'd almost forgot since I was running for my life but, I remember. His light was maybe the brightest I've ever seen."

"Yes, and you need to meet him, now," Abdiel said with authority and concern in his voice.

"But why?"

Abdiel took a deep breath, hoping his words wouldn't induce too much fear in Anne as fear, especially intense fear was like a beacon to demons. "I have been sent to protect you from those in my world, but I have little influence over yours. There are men, bad men, followers of the darkness that are looking for you."

Anne was more surprised than fearful. "What? How? Nobody even knows who I am, or where I am for that matter."

Abdiel shook his head. "The demons know who you are now and that you have abilities beyond any human. They have undoubtedly given that information to Lucifer's followers here in the city."

Now the fear crept in. "Here? In New Orleans? How? Are there others that see like me? Is this man supposed to protect me from them?"

Abdiel moved back towards the street and motioned for Anne to follow. "Yes, his guardian is working to keep him here so that he may guard you in your world where I cannot."

The Angel waved his hand around.

"There are followers of wickedness everywhere and in this city in particular. And no, I have never met or heard of another with sight like yours. It is a unique gift. These people seek communion with demons through ancient methods and witchcraft, giving over their souls for the hope of some power in their world. It is a fickle bargain that will cost them in the end."

Anne looked down as she followed Abdiel to the street. She whispered softly, as to not draw any attention. "What happens to them?"

Abdiel looked at Anne for a moment before pointing to an emaciated charred demon several feet away standing close to a large man who was visibly very angry.

"That is what awaits them. Those that take pleasure in the pain

55

of others will suffer far more than they can imagine before continuing their dark service. The only respite from their pain is feeding off the negative energy of others sewing more chaos and hate," the guardian sorrowfully looked down to Anne. "Lucifer's armies far outnumber our own as the world falls further and further away from Father. Every guardian knows the pain of losing one to the enemy and as deep as that pain is it is nothing compared to the pain Father feels when his children fall to darkness."

Intense sadness overcame Anne as Abdiel's words sunk into her core. After a moment of what felt like mourning for the world, she changed the subject and asked, "So where is this man?"

Abdiel pointed to a diner on the opposite corner from where they were standing.

Anne looked at Abdiel, "Wait, he's in there?"

The Angel nodded.

Anne looked out the corner of her eyes as a thought occurred to her, "Wait, I didn't get here by chance, did I?"

Abdiel shook his head slowly. "No, you did not."

Anne laughed a bit. "But how? I don't remember anything bringing me here."

"Thank you, that means I did my job well."

The angel smiled. "Come, the Spirit is telling me we need to move now."

"The Spirit?" Anne pondered aloud.

Abdiel led the young lady to the crosswalk with a wry smile. He loved her inquisitiveness, but he had to keep her on task.

"Later."

* * *

Anne entered the Grill Pit diner and slowly looked around. The smell of eggs, sausage, and buttered grits hanging in the air reminded her stomach that it had been a full twenty-four hours since her last meal. She searched the diner until she spotted the man she was sent to find. It wasn't difficult as his light shone brighter than everyone else in the restaurant.

"Just you ma'am?" a middle-aged waitress asked, drawing Anne's attention.

"Uh, no, I'm joining someone. Right there," Anne pointed to the man in the corner booth.

The waitress had a strong but sweet, playful voice, "Oh honey, good thing you showed up or I was about to steal your man. He's got some dreamy eyes!"

Anne couldn't help but blush a little, unsure of her response. "Yeah... he sure does."

"Go ahead sugar, what you want to drink?" the waitress asked.

"Just water please," Anne answered.

"Okay baby, I'll have that right to ya. Menus on the table, hun. I'm Gigi, just holla if you need sumthin," she said with a smile.

"Thank you," Anne said as Gigi moved away.

She slowly made her way to the man sitting at the table. He was a large man around thirty with broad shoulders and an athletic build. He was clean cut with short brown hair, but his facial hair looked like it was overdue for a shave. He had a pair of reading glasses on and was studying a small book with a leather binding that lay next to his cup of coffee.

Anne approached the table and paused momentarily, causing him to look up as she sat in the booth across from him. Immediately the man closed the book and removed his reading glasses.

"Do I know you?" he said.

He thought he recognized the young woman but wasn't sure.

Anne squinted as she tried to focus through the man's light onto his face. After a moment she was able to see his blue eyes, "Gigi was right, you do have pretty eyes."

The man was confused, "Uh..."

Gigi walked up with Anne's water, "You know what you want hun or you need a minute?"

Anne felt around in her pocket, "How much for an order of eggs?" She asked as she leaned over, pulling a dollar and some change out of her pocket.

"$3.99 with toast, $2.99 for just the eggs," Gigi answered.

Anne counted out the 3.48 from she still had from yesterday, she wasn't able to find any more with everything that had happened. "How much are the eggs after tax?"

Gigi could see the young woman looked hungry and embarrassed as she was counting out her change. She was about to tell her not to worry about it and bring her the eggs and toast when the gentleman spoke up.

"Get her whatever she wants," he said calmly.

Anne was even more embarrassed. "No, it's okay, I've got some money. Thank you, though."

The man picked up the menu resting between the saltshakers and the napkin holder, "You eat meat, right?" he asked as he looked over the menu to her subtle nod. "Get her the steak and eggs please with coffee, or whatever she'd like to drink."

Gigi felt warm at the goodness coming from the man, but downplayed it as to not embarrass the girl, "Good choice! How would you like your steak and eggs, baby?"

59

Anne looked at the man for a moment, then back to Gigi. "Scrambled, please, and medium-rare."

"Grits or hash browns, and toast or biscuit?" Gigi asked.

"Grits and biscuit please," Anne smiled.

"You got it, sugar."

As Gigi was about to walk away the man spoke up, "I'd like a Grit too, please."

Gigi turned around, "Just one, baby?"

Anne covered her face as both she and Gigi giggled. Anne spoke through her amusement, "You're not from the south, are you?"

Gigi walked over and put a hand on the man's shoulder. "It's alright, sugar, Mama Giselle's gonna fix you right up."

She winked and walked off to put in the order.

Both Anne and the man met eyes for a moment as they both went to speak at the same time.

"Who are-"

"Thank you."

The man shook his head. "It's nothing, but um, who are you? You look familiar, but I don't know where from."

Anne bit her lower lip a bit. "I um... kinda ran into you yesterday at the cathedral."

The man's eyes grew big. "Yes, I remember. Are you okay? You seemed really scared."

"That's a very loaded question," Anne said, thinking to herself of all that had transpired since their encounter. "In a way, I'm better than I've ever been. Yet...." Anne held up a finger, "I'm apparently in mortal danger, which is why I was sent to you."

The man rubbed his temples. This woman looked normal and was beautiful even through her tattered clothes, but she was obviously not right in the head.

"Is there something I can help you with?" he asked.

Anne took a breath as she looked at the man. "What's your name? I think we should probably start there."

He looked at Anne curiously.

"John," he said flatly.

"No, it's not," Abdiel manifested standing next to the booth. "It's William."

"Turner," a deep voice with an accent that sounded distinctly African said as the guardian manifested across from Abdiel. "William Turner."

Chapter 4: The Guardians

Rahim was a twiceborn guardian angel. Born in Egypt, Rahim was raised in the teachings of Moses handed down through his grandfather. A very imposing man, he stood as a giant of the times with dark skin, long braided hair, and a thick black beard. Though he was gifted with great natural strength and was sought after often as a warrior, it was his pure heart and great deeds on earth of charity and love that caught God's attention. Rahim was not martyred like so many Saints. He was not a prophet or great teacher, but he spent every moment of his life in the service of others.

One evening a fire engulfed a large village that Rahim was passing through on his pilgrimage east. While everyone feared the flames, it was Rahim who rushed into home after home, using his great strength to tear down walls and carry the villagers to safety. He fought with every breath to save every person he could. It was on his last trip that he dropped off three children to crying and grateful parents when he turned to go back. With his skin charred, his hair singed and his lungs reaching their capacity for smoke, Rahim fell. Because of his sacrifice, none of the villagers died that night.

It is said that when one dies in the service of others that Father himself comes to take them home.

Anne looked up to the large angel standing beside William. "Wow, you're a big one."

Rahim stood tall in his white robes and golden armor. He wore a half chest piece over his left side and beautiful vambraces. His robes were tan with a beautiful multicolored sash that looked out of place. He looked at Anne confused as she looked right at him.

Abdiel looked at him. "We need to talk, brother."

William looked to his left but saw no one there. He really was sitting with a crazy person.

Gigi walked up with their order. "Here y'all go, enjoy!"

William looked down into his bowl of grits with a melted chunk of butter on top. He then looked at Anne, who had her sole focus on filling her ravenous appetite."

"Thank you so much, William! I can't remember the last time I've had such a great meal."

William froze, he knew he didn't tell this woman his real name. Any other person would have completely freaked out, but William immediately became concerned that demons influenced the woman, something he had dealt with before.

"In the name of Jesus, I command you demon to tell me your name," William said in a low but authoritative voice as he inadvertently reached for the cross around his neck.

Anne stopped mid shovel and almost spit out her food. "Um, no... sorry..."

She looked to the Guardian Angels standing to her right.

"How am I supposed to do this?"

Rahim was still trying to figure out what was going on while Abdiel just shook his head, "I leave this to you."

Anne slowly nodded as she cut a piece of her steak. "Okay, what the hell."

She put it in her mouth and began to talk once it was chewed a bit.

"Oh man, so good. Okay, so good news, I'm not a demon but I *can* see them."

William continued to stare at the woman, not knowing what to think as she spoke in between bites.

"I see Angels too. I have my whole life. Well, not like I see them now, they used to be little wisps of light, but the point is I can see *their* world and communicate with them. And my Angel Abdiel, he's right here, told me that I needed to find you so you can protect me from the bad guys who want me for something."

Anne continued enjoying her breakfast as she spoke through a full mouth.

"Oh, Turner is your last name?"

"Is she supposed to be telling him these things?" Rahim anxiously asked Abdiel. "We are going to get into trouble, Father is not going to be happy."

Abdiel put his hands out. "No, no, it's fine I spoke with the Lamb, everything is okay."

Rahim's eyes got wide. "No, no, it is not okay! Who is this woman who can see and hear me? Jesus says this is okay. Are you sure?"

Anne turned to Rahim. "Hey, relax. This is all new to me too. I mean, look at him," she nodded towards William. "He is freaking out right now."

Rahim looked at Abdiel, who could have sworn he was getting a headache even though he'd never had one before, "Relax? Relax! I have to go to the Lamb!"

Abdiel nodded, "Probably for the best."

And with that, Rahim vanished.

Anne looked up at Abdiel. "I don't know who's taking it worse."

Abdiel just shook his head.

William was so befuddled. He really didn't know what to think. "So, you are saying that you communicate with... angels?"

Anne took a moment to swallow her food, then in a breath, her tone became more serious. "I know it sounds crazy, I-"

Anne put her fork down and pushed her plate away. She took a long, deep breath.

"Imagine you're a child that has always seen spirits and wisps of light and dark everywhere you went, seeing everyone's head glowing one or the other telling you if they are good or bad. Imagine that everyone you told called you crazy and the ones you loved the most had you hospitalized where you were medicated and tortured by endless pain and darkness around that only you could see."

Anne's jovial attitude was gone as she revealed the sadness of her life.

"Well, that was me. Running my whole life trying to find some small bit of peace. Then, yesterday I began to see the wisps for what they were," Anne looked at William, trying to not let her initial fear overcome her. "When I ran into you yesterday, I was running from a demon, a disgusting, horrible thing that chased me."

William listened intently, hearing Anne's words and feeling energy pulsing through his body as shivers.

"I have never been more afraid in my life, and last night more of them chased me... until I prayed." Anne looked to Abdiel standing next to her with tears of gratitude and love forming in her eyes, "Then my guardian angel came."

Anne wiped a tear falling down her cheek as she laughed.

"And he kicked their butts!"

Abdiel smiled at Anne with love flowing through him. Most humans had no idea the battles Angel's fight for them every day, and although they never sought credit, to be acknowledged touched Abdiel's heart.

"And now, apparently these demons have told some men in our world about me and they are coming for me."

She looked deep into William's eyes.

"My Angel met with Jesus, he is who sent us here to you, William."

William was overwhelmed with what Anne had told him. He never took his eyes off of her as he felt a gentle pressure on his left temple.

Anne slowly pulled her plate back. "I can't make you beli-"

"I believe you," William said as he looked into Anne's emerald eyes. "I... have never told anyone this but, I *feel* things. Intuition, I guess. I am a very faithful man and whenever I feel particularly close to God, I feel pressure," William moved his finger to his left temple. "I feel it right here."

At that moment, Rahim materialized next to William with his index and middle fingers touching William's left temple.

Anne smiled as she looked at the large Angel who smiled back to her, "I am sorry, this is a very unique situation," Rahim then looked to Abdiel. "I should have trusted you, my brother."

Abdiel shook his head. "You should have seen the state of panic I was in when I found out."

William saw Anne smiling up, "You see them now?"

Anne looked back at him. "Yes! The reason you felt that pressure is because your guardian was touching you there."

Rahim looked to Abdiel. "I do not know what to do. If she can see and hear all, I am afraid to speak. What if I say something she is not meant to know? What if she tells him something that alters his path?"

Abdiel held his hands outward. "I had the same concern, but the Lamb reassured me that this, Anne, all of us, our paths are intertwined and that we should trust Father as he trusts us."

With that, a visible sense of calm washed over Rahim as he nodded and smiled slightly. "Anne, please tell William that the reason I am able to connect with him like this is because of his faith and connection to Father."

Anne smiled, happy to relay Rahim's message. "Your angel says that the reason he is able to connect with you is because of your faith and connection to Father."

William sat up, truly humbled. Tears began to form in his eyes now. "Jesus sent you... to *me*?"

While William was dumbstruck, the other three beamed in pride.

After a few moments, William was able to gather his thoughts. "Did he tell you anything about me? About who I am and what I do?"

Anne shook her head as she took a sip of her coffee. "Nope," she met eyes with Abdiel, who also shook his head. "What do you do?"

William leaned back in his seat. "It's complicated."

* * *

"Pull over here," Sebastian said to Tripp Romero, who was driving the well-tinted grey SUV.

Junior turned around to watch Sebastian in the back seat. Laney Broussard Jr. was raised in the lodge. His Father was already lodgemaster when he was born and so he was brought up looking at those who weren't members of his organization as beneath him. Slaves to be used and cattle to be slaughtered. So, when one of the "profane" joins, ascends, and excels at connecting to the veil the way Sebastian has, it drew great envy from the

69

lodgemaster's son.

Junior was a good-looking and clean-cut man of twenty-five with brown eyes and well-kept sandy blonde hair that was parted to the side. He was dressed in khakis and a polo shirt.

"Why is this girl so damned important, anyway?" Junior asked with vitriol in his voice.

Sebastian held up a hand for quiet as he let the weight of his pendulum drop.

Junior huffed as Sebastian yelled at the large man in the front seat, "Keep still!"

After a moment of complete stillness, the pendulum began to circle until it slowly began to swing in a diagonal direction. Sebastian slowly looked in the direction indicated by the demon.

"Is she in the coffee shop?" He asked as the demon swayed the pendulum side to side, indicating no.

"Is she in the antique store?" Sebastian asked as he moved down the row of businesses.

Sebastian looked to the last place the pendulum was pointed to and asked, "Is she in the diner?"

The pendulum circled straight and began to swing wildly backward and forward. Sebastian met eyes with Junior and Tripp.

"We need to identify her first, then we can follow her."

"Well, I can eat," Tripp said in a deep mongoloid voice.

Junior rolled his eyes.

"When can't you eat?" he said in an aggravated tone.

The trio exited the SUV as Sebastian pocketed his pendulum. "She is a young woman with red hair, her name is Anne."

"Hopefully there aint too many redheads in there, huh," Tripp said.

Junior took the lead as he walked across the street. "Don't look too hard Tripp, we don't need you giving us away again."

The six-foot three, three hundred plus pound man was a little wounded but kept his mouth shut as they made their way to the diner.

* * *

Anne looked at William curiously. She didn't know anything about this man, only that his light shone very bright.

"Well, what's your story? I mean, it can't be any crazier than mine!" Anne said with a lifted brow.

William cocked his head a bit. "I've never told anyone my *story*, hell only a handful of people actually know my real name."

71

Anne didn't say anything but looked at him with a stern, un-blinking resolve.

William nodded. "Okay, I never knew my parents, only that they died shortly after I was born. I was raised by...." he paused for a moment trying to gather the words, "I was raised by a group, a kind of religious order."

"A cult?" Anne asked in a concerned tone.

William shook his head as answered a bit defensively. "No, not a cult. My order has been around for a long time but recently our primary..."

William picked a seat facing the entrance of the diner as he was trained to do. Ever since Anne had told him that men were looking for her, he had subconsciously been watching everyone who entered. Three men walked in the door and immediately started surveying the place. One looked like a Saints lineman, one a sales agent, and the other looked like an older college student.

Anne saw William's attention shift and turned her head to the three.

"Turn around, look at me," William said in a stern but calm voice.

Anne's eyes grew big as she turned back.

"William, there is darkness all around them!" she said nervously.

William nodded. "Stay calm, okay."

Anne swallowed the lump in her throat and nodded.

"Can you see anything else with them?" he asked.

Anne hadn't seen any demons initially, but she knew they were there.

Rahim spoke to Anne as both he and Abdiel watched the trio. "Do not fear young one. William will protect you. I promise, no demon will accost you this day."

Abdiel's demeanor changed almost instantly into that of a warrior ready for battle. "Anne, as soon as I tell you to you and William must leave through the back door."

Anne looked around. "I don't see a back door."

Neither guardian took their eyes off the three men as Rahim spoke. "It is through the kitchen door behind me."

Anne nodded and met eyes with William. "We have to leave through the kitchen as soon as they tell us."

* * *

Gigi met the men at the register and began leading them to their seats all the while they surveyed the place for Anne.

Unfortunately, her red hair stood out amongst the other patrons, making it easy for Sebastian to identify her. The men took their seats and ordered drinks. After Gigi left, they spoke in hushed tones.

"She's over there. There's a man with her," Sebastian said.

Junior was aggravated. "You didn't say anything about a man."

Sebastian turned low to the corner of the booth and pulled his pendulum to once again commune with demons.

After a moment, he looked up. "That is her, they know nothing of the man."

* * *

"Go now," Abdiel said with authority.

Anne looked at William. "Okay, we have to go now."

William stood up, reached for his wallet and laid $60 on the table then stood to the side, and motioned for Anne to go. Just before he moved to follow her, he met eyes with Sebastian and ever so subtly shook his head. In that short moment, William hoped to convey a clear and simple message.

"*Don't*"

He then turned and followed Anne through the employees-only door.

"Damnit, they're on to us! Tripp, go around the front, we'll follow out back," Sebastian said as he was already in motion.

Junior was confused. "What? How? They don't even know we're here," he said neither him nor Tripp moving from their seat.

Sebastian leaned over the table and spoke through gritted teeth. "Fine, you explain to your father how you let her get away!"

He then turned and moved toward the kitchen door.

Junior grunted as he yelled at Tripp, "Go around back now!"

Tripp moved with a purpose as Junior followed Sebastian.

Anne paused for a moment and William grabbed her hand as he moved by the kitchen staff as if he knew where he was going. He led her to the back door, which was already open as a delivery was being made.

"This way," William moved outside and alongside the building, trying to find an escape.

They passed a couple of employees sitting on milk crates as they smoked, who looked confused.

Sebastian and Junior hastened their pace fast enough to see the plastic strips hanging on the back door moving from their prey passing through.

William and Anne rounded the corner of the building making

their way to the main street hoping to get lost in the crowd but before they got there Tripp stepped out.

As large as William was, Tripp was much bigger. Both he and Anne stopped in their tracks as William pushed Anne behind him.

"William!" Anne cried out as Sebastian and Junior had just turned the corner.

William looked behind for a moment as he assessed the situation. He watched as Tripp began to reach under his shirt.

He smirked ever so slightly as he looked at the big man just a few paces away. "Are you sure you want to do that?"

"William, they're here! Oh God, there are so many of them."

There was a total of eight demons with Sebastian and Junior, each as vile and disgusting as the ones Anne encountered the night before. To make matters worse, she could sense more with the large man in front of William. Something was different in Anne this time. She didn't quite understand why, but she wasn't afraid.

The lead demon was tall with tight skin the color of embers and two black horns jutting from his head. Anne was about to say a prayer, but before she could, Rahim materialized directly in front of the tall demon with his hand around its throat. With a blur and flash of his wings, the large Angel threw the demon to the side and into Abdiel's ethereal scimitar, which pierced the creature's neck all the way through.

As the demon turned to ash, the others ran at Rahim.

William quickly moved in as the large man reached for his gun. Before Tripp could draw it up, the mysterious Mr. Turner grabbed the gun with both hands and shoulder charged him. William then quickly used the man's momentum to rotate the gun outside, disarming Tripp and firing instinctively with two shots to his chest.

Anne jumped at the sudden gunshots as William yelled, "Down!"

He immediately turned and opened fire on Sebastian and Junior, who ducked around the back of the building before they had time to draw their own guns.

Abdiel dematerialized and teleported behind the group of demons dipping low slicing their legs in a spin before slicing upward, cleaving one from hip to neck.

Rahim moved like a large lightning bolt as he materialized two glowing chains that wrapped his wrists, each with a bladed spearhead on the end. He flashed across the alley in a blur, pausing only for a moment as his chains tore through demon flesh.

Anne watched as the two guardians decimated Lucifer's minions with only momentary sparks as their weapons met. Her ears were ringing from the gunshots and screaming on the street as William grabbed her hand.

77

"Come on!" he yelled, pulling her away and down the street. "Run!"

Anne followed William as they ran down the street, turning only for a second to see Abdiel throw a demon to the ground and pierce his skull with two glowing blades that materialized from his fist.

The duo turned down a street as the fleeing crowd began to spread and sirens were heard. He took apart the gun and proceeded to drop the pieces in storm drains as they passed. Eventually, they began to walk as to not draw any attention.

After several minutes of relative calm, Anne stopped.

"William... wait!" she said as she tried to catch her breath.

William stopped and looked around to survey the area.

"Are you okay?" he asked.

Anne nodded. "Yeah, but... William, you killed that man."

William nodded. "I know. It was a reaction. He drew on us and instinct just kicked in," he looked around to check their location. "I know a safe place we can go."

Anne nodded as he led her away. "You... Who are you, William?"

William met her eyes for a moment as he surveyed the area. "Like I was saying, my parents died when I was young, I don't remember much about them, just flashes here and there. I had no other family to speak of. None that were close anyway. My parents, they were devout Catholics, and our family priest was my godfather. He arranged for my... care."

He paused for a moment in thought as he looked down. Anne looked worryingly at William, who eased her concerns.

"No, nothing like that. It was a good place. I was sent to Scotland for a while, then France, and then eventually Philadelphia."

William turned to Anne. "What do you know of the Knights Templar?"

Anne thought for a moment, "They were crusaders, right? Didn't they protect the roads to the holy land? I think I saw that in a documentary once."

William smiled. "Very good! Yes, that's true, they also created the world's first banking system among many other things, but what's more important is what's not known."

The couple made their way across the street as William continued, "So, the Templars were infiltrated by a group of..."

William sighed.

"Luciferians. There was a rift in the order that predates the purge of 1307 by at least two hundred years. A small subset of Templars broke off and stayed true to our original doctrine."

Anne looked up at William. "So, you're a Templar?" she asked.

William took a breath. "My order is the Templars Fidei, Templars of Faith. We hold to the original teachings of Christ, although our mission has changed considerably over the last five hundred years."

The two continued down the street close to the cathedral, where they bumped into each other less than a day before.

"So, what is your *mission*? I'm no expert but I saw the way you took down that man, did the Templars teach you that?" Anne asked.

"Templars Fidei, we don't want to be mistaken for them and no, I didn't learn that in the order. Our mission had become such that we needed specialists in our rankings. At nineteen I was chosen to join the army, I worked very hard, became Airborne, and eventually a green beret. After eight years, I returned to Philadelphia and began my work."

William met eyes with Anne as he really didn't like sharing this information, but he could see she wouldn't relent, plus he figured the Angels could tell her, anyway.

"The primary objective of the Templars Fidei is to find and shut down the varying branches of the Luciferian Knights Templar," he stopped for a moment and looked at the church now in view. "My job, is to track down and eliminate Baal cultists."

Anne shook her head, never hearing the name.

"Baal?" she asked.

William took a deep breath. "One of the many offshoots of devil worship, this one, in particular, specializes in the trafficking, abuse, and sacrifice of children."

Anne covered her mouth in horror, she had no words as she was overcome with sadness. Whatever reservations she felt when William said his job was to "eliminate" were gone as she was suddenly even more grateful for this man.

William looked down. He was not proud of what he did, but he carried no guilt for removing such evil from the world. These men viewed any who were not like them as cattle, and William viewed any who would harm a child as less than human.

"I was here investigating a lead, but the trail went cold. I was supposed to leave out yesterday on a flight to Denver, but my flight was delayed," William looked at Anne and smiled. "Three times."

He began walking again. "I knew God was keeping me here for a reason but..."

He kept smiling as he looked at Anne. She was beautiful by any man's standards as the breeze blew her red locks across her face.

"Never in a million years would I have guessed... you."

Anne looked up and smiled back, her cheeks blushing a bit. "C'mon, don't pretend I'm the first girl you ever met that told you Jesus sent her."

William bit his lip a bit as he chuckled. "The priest at this cathedral is one of my order, he is a good man. We can hide out here a while."

"Father Daniel!" Anne said excitedly.

William cocked his head. "You know him?"

Anne smiled as she thought of Father Daniels' kindness. "He's a sweet man."

The two made their way up the steps where they met and into the church. Across the street stood a seemingly normal man watching them. Azazel watched with his dark eyes fixated on his prize.

He spoke softly aloud, "*You will serve me girl, or you will suffer me.*"

Chapter 5: Seeking exodus

Sheriff Landry was devastated as he angrily chased away re-porters from the crime scene. His only son, Tripp Landry, was shot and killed in a robbery.

Of course, he knew the truth, but he couldn't tell the press that his son was sent to abduct a girl and was shot in the act. So, Tripp's friends tearfully recounted the story of how a black man shot and robbed him, nearly murdering them in the process.

Sheriff Landry only said one thing to Junior and Sebastian, "Tell Broussard I want him, he can have whatever resources he needs, but when you fiend the son of a bitch who did this you bring him to me, yah understand?"

Both men simply nodded.

Tripp was Junior's best friend, he went to school with him, had known him his whole life.

"That dumbass!" he said as he and Sebastian walked back to the SUV. "Why did he even get that close!" Junior then turned his anger on Sebastian. "And who the hell is this girl you got him killed for?"

The lodgemaster's son continued on an expletive-filled tirade for almost a full minute until Sebastian had finally had enough. He reached across the center console, grabbed Junior's neck, and slammed him three times into the passenger side door.

"Shut up!" he screamed as Junior froze in terror, never seeing Sebastian lose his temper.

Sebastian pulled Junior close as he spoke with anger and vitriol. "I know you think this is just some good ole boy club that your daddy runs so your spoiled ass can just run around and do what you want and that's fine but let me make something perfectly clear!"

Sebastian leaned even closer towards Junior's ear.

"I don't serve you or your arrogant father, and the orders I receive come directly from my master."

Sebastian released Junior in almost a throw as he returned to his seat. "Tripp was an idiot and died because of his own stupidity."

Junior was near tears. As hard as he pretended to be, he had a close relationship with Tripp that no one else was aware of.

Sebastian rolled his eyes at Junior's weakness. "I need to commune with master and find out where they are hiding, and I need some peace. Go call your *daddy* and tell him I need brothers on standby, preferably trained ones who know how to handle themselves."

Sebastian looked Junior up and down with disgust. "Get out!"

* * *

A peace came over William and Anne as they entered the church. This time Anne followed William's lead by crossing herself with holy water as they walked towards the alter.

"John, I didn't think I would see you again for some time!" Father Daniel said to William, then he noticed Anne. "And you, young lady, how are you?" he asked with a smile.

This time Anne was not timid as she moved past William. "I'm... " she looked back at William to see that Rahim and Abdiel had joined them, then back to Father Daniel with a small chuckle. "Father things are even crazier than when I was here yesterday, but somehow..." Anne gave the purest smile of peace. "Things are okay, no... things are better than okay."

The look on Anne's face brought joy to Father Daniel's heart. He remembered how the poor girl was suffering only the day before but there was no mistaking that something had shifted in her.

William however looked at her as if she was crazy. Just a few hours ago he was sitting in a diner waiting to get a call back about his flight when this petite redhead just sits at his table and changes his life.

85

He looked at Father Daniel. "I wouldn't say things are that okay."

He waited for a moment as a parishioner passed them on her way out and then spoke in hushed tones.

"Father, we're in a bit of a jam and need a place to lie low for a while."

Father Daniel nodded as he thought for a moment. "For how long? I can set you up in a..."

"No, Father, I can't say why, but it would be really good if we could stay here until tomorrow. We'll leave in the morning, by that time things should be okay and hopefully I'll have a plan," William said as he looked behind Father Daniel to Sister Helen who was eyeing the three suspiciously.

Father Daniel thought for a moment. "It's only lunchtime, there's not much to do. Might get pretty bored."

Anne shrugged. "It's fine, do you have a deck of cards? We'll just play go fish or something."

Father Daniel shook his head.

"Not with Sister Helen around."

The Priest once again turned to make eye contact with the nun and waved.

"No way she'd allow playing cards in here, 'they is tha devil.' She caught me last week playing bingo and actually called me a Judas," Father Daniel said with a shocked expression. "I mean, they assign me to New Orleans and expect me not to have a little fun?"

He looked back to Sister Helen, thankfully far enough away not to hear.

"I don't think God's going to condemn my soul to eternal damnation for some beignets and bingo."

Anne turned as she heard Rahim's deep laugh. "Beignet's and bingo."

Anne could hardly hold her chuckle at how funny Rahim sounded saying those words.

"We won't be a bother, Father. You won't even know we're here."

Father Daniel nodded.

"Hopefully, no one else will either," he said with a wink.

* * *

It had taken hours, but Sebastian was finally able to find where the girl and man were hiding. He and Junior were parked across the street from the entrance of the Cathedral when a sheriff's car pulled behind them. Sheriff Landry got out and approached the driver's side. Junior rolled down the window.

"You sure they're in there?" he asked Junior, who looked over to Sebastian.

"They're in there, sheriff," Sebastian said with confidence.

Sheriff Landry stood up for a moment and looked around, the evening sun glimmering in his aviators.

"Okay, the back is covered. There's no way they're getting out of there without one of us seeing them," he leaned back in the window. "We'll let this traffic clear out, let it get dark and if they aint out yet we're going in to get them!"

Sebastian nodded. "That's fine with us Sheriff, you can have the man, but we ne-"

"I know, I know, you get the girl," Sheriff Landry said with slight irritation.

Sebastian smiled as the Sheriff moved back to his patrol car and drove off.

Sebastian didn't care for Landry, he was just another dirty politician who got everything in life based on his family connections. He did, however, like the resources he provided.

He looked across Junior and towards the church. Soon he would fulfill his master's will, and he knew his reward would be great.

* * *

Anne was on the phone while William went over their travel plans in his notebook.

"Yes, thick crust, half with everything and the other half just pepperoni," she moved a little away from William and whispered a bit into the phone. "Is the delivery driver there? Oh, you are. Look, I'll give you an extra ten if you can bring a deck of cards. Yeah, no, that's fine, okay. Yeah, if you're looking at the front doors, follow around the left side of the building till you see a door. I'll be there. Awesome, thank you!"

William gave Anne $40 and told her to order whatever she wanted. Father Daniel was right, Anne was bored. She thought William would have a ton of questions, but he was just focused on planning their escape from New Orleans. She figured she could just chat with Abdiel and Rahim, but they haven't *appeared* for several hours, although she knew they were around.

She hung up the phone and turned to William. "So, this is a nun's room, huh?"

Father Daniel had to fight with Sister Helen to take a couple of days in a nice hotel, she was a very pious woman.

Take a couple of days, Sister, enjoy yourself! he said, eventually ordering her, which definitely didn't go over well.

William looked around the room, which held a desk, chair, twin bed, and small dresser. A cross hung over the bed and a rather graphic painting of Christ crucified hung on the wall. Anne's eyes fixated on it, uncomfortable with the image.

"I hate it," William said flatly.

Anne looked at him, confused.

"I mean, I'm grateful, but I hate seeing him like that. It just... hurts, doesn't seem right."

Anne cocked her head. "What do you mean?"

William looked at the image. "That's just not what the image that comes to mind when I think of Jesus. I know, he did that for us, but when I close my eyes all I see is a man. He looks so normal, his hair is brown, his skin is darkened and rough from the sun. He's clothed in the simplest of robes, and he's walking with several people around. Then, he stops for just a moment and looks at me."

Anne watched as William's light grew with every pulse until it lit the whole room making it hard for her to look at him, but she didn't turn away.

Tears formed in William's closed eyes as he continued.

"He turns and gives just a subtle smile but, I feel... The love I feel from him it's incredible, it's the realist thing I've ever felt!" William opened his eyes and wiped them. "I don't know why that image moves me so much but, *that* is how I see him."

He looked up again at the image.

"I believe that, but it's the image of Jesus smiling at me that just... Feels right."

Everything was silent for a moment, then Anne spoke up through a sniffle as she too was moved by William's image.

"I'm gonna go check for the pizza guy."

"I'll go with you," William said as he began to get up from the desk.

"I'll be okay, it's literally six feet away," she said with a small amount of snark.

William looked at her, not quite happy with her response but happy that she wasn't afraid like she told him she was her whole life.

"Okay, but leave the door open."

"You got it, Kevin Costner," she said to which William was confused as he wasn't much of a movie enthusiast and had never seen, "The Bodyguard."

Sister Helen's room bordered on the room used for Sunday school, which is where the back door to the cathedral was. Along the wall was a line of windows which made it easy to see outside. Anne saw the pizza guy walking past the windows and met him at the door. His light quelled any nervousness she may have had as she opened the door.

"Hi!" she said hungrily.

"Hi, it's $18.53, and I got your cards right here," the pizza guy said with a wink.

Anne smiled and gave him the $40 as she took the pizza. "Awesome! Thank you so much. Keep, the change."

The pizza guy was very happy. "Oh wow, thank you so much."

Anne was happy to have the privilege of being the bearer of William's generosity, she knew too well what it was to live off the charity of others.

The pizza man turned to leave as Anne moved to come inside. When she turned to shut the door, her heart sank as she dropped the pizza.

William heard the noise and flew to her as she was stepping back in terror. Her lips moved, but no words came out.

"What's wrong?" William couldn't see anything as Anne looked into the street surrounding the church.

She backed into him as he moved to her side, trying to read her lips as the words slowly began to form. "Abdiel, Abdiel, Abdiel, Abdiel!"

William looked again seeing nothing out of the ordinary, then turned to stand directly in front of Anne. "What do you see?"

Abdiel and Rahim immediately appeared behind William, looking out onto the area surrounding the church.

"Anne!" William said, finally getting her attention.

She looked at him, her lips trembling. "They're... They're out there."

William looked again, then looked back. "Demons?"

Anne nodded. "Yes... Hundreds of them."

* * *

Father Daniel stepped out of his room next to Sister Helen's, dressed in jogging pants, a sweatshirt, and furry slippers. "What's the matter?"

William turned to him for a moment. "Father... I..."

Father Daniel could see William wanted to tell him something and could see even more how distraught Anne was. He closed the open back door and began to lower the blinds on all the windows. He then came back to William and Anne.

"Okay, what is going on? She obviously knows your real name, what else have you told her?" Father Daniel asked specifically wondering if Anne knew about the Templars Fidei.

William looked at Anne, who was still unnerved. "Father, I never told her my name."

Father Daniel was perplexed as he tilted his head. "What?"

Anne looked at the guardian standing next to him. She was tall and beautiful with flowing blonde hair that piercing gray-blue eyes. She reminded Anne of Galadriel from the Lord of The Rings.

The angel looked at Anne, not as surprised as Rahim and Abdiel were, but she didn't look completely comfortable either.

The angel looked at Abdiel, who nodded. She then turned and spoke to Anne.

"Tell him that under the false bottom of his trunk he keeps a photo of his first love, a stale pack of half-used cigarettes, and a Micky Mantle rookie card his father gave him on his fourteenth birthday.

Anne nodded slightly and tried to compose herself as she relayed the message. "Your guardian angel says that in the false bottom of your chest are some stale cigarettes, a baseball card your father gave you on your fourteenth birthday, and a picture of your first love."

Father Daniels' eyes got wide as he stepped back, nearly falling over a desk in the classroom.

"Father!" William grabbed Father Daniel and helped him to sit in a chair that looked far too small for him.

"I... I... you... but how?" The priest's rational thought told him she must have gone through his things, but how could she know his dad gave him that card and when.

William took a deep breath, "Father, Anne sees the spirit world and the beings in it. She has her entire life. She can see and hear angels... and demons."

There was a long silence in the room that was broken by Abdiel. "Anne, look at me."

Anne turned with tears in her eyes.

"Do you trust me?" he said to her with a loving smile.

William and Father Daniel watched as Anne wiped tears from her eyes as she nodded to whom they could not see.

"Then trust this, in the name of the Father I say unto you, no demon shall harm you. I have been with you from the beginning and I will be with you until the end, and after."

In Father's kingdom, there was no greater show of love than an embrace. Abdiel wanted more than anything to wrap his arms around Anne and comfort her.

Then Father Daniel stood up. "I... you... *This* is why you were so upset yesterday," he said with watering eyes.

Anne nodded slowly as she wiped her tears away.

"The burden you carry, my child," Father Daniel said with his arms open.

Anne fell into his arms, crying on his chest as he held her. Even with angels around, we need to feel safe, to be embraced in safety and comfort. Anne wished so long for the protective embrace of a father. She laid in Father Daniel's arms for a long while.

William didn't want to disrupt, but he needed to assess the situation they were in. He peeked through the blinds to get a detailed look at the cars parked across the street. He noticed one that had at least two men sitting in it and another with dark tinted windows he thought looked out of place. He checked the deadbolt on the door before turning to Anne and Father Daniel.

"There are men watching the church, we have to check the front," he said in a calm but assertive tone.

Father Daniel tilted his head back as he looked at Anne and gave the subtlest of nods. "Come on, we'll make sure everything is secure."

No one else was in the cathedral as it closed over an hour ago. All six made their way to the front, William checking the confessional among other places someone might hide.

"William!" Anne shouted a bit louder than she intended to as she peaked through the small windows on the side of the large wooden doors.

William ran quickly and looked out the small window as he stood behind Anne. "Same as the back door. I'm thinking there are somewhere around ten men watching this place."

He then asked Anne, "What do you see?"

Anne looked out as she surveyed the area. "William, they are everywhere... Even more than the back door!" She then turned to Abdiel. "You said they can't harm us, right? The demons, that they only have the power *we* give them."

Father Daniel looked to where Abdiel was standing but of course, could see nothing.

Abdiel looked to Rahim and Yelena, Father Daniels guardian, then back to Anne. "Yesterday you were unsure, afraid," Abdiel smiled slightly. "Have you ever wondered why you cannot see your own light?"

Actually, Anne had wondered this her whole life. She could see the spirit world even reflected in water, so why when she looked at herself in the mirror couldn't she see hers. She looked at Abdiel, perplexed.

"None of Father's children can see their own light," Rahim said in a matter-of-fact tone as Abdiel and Yelena shared reassuring glances.

Yelena looked at Anne and smiled as she spoke in the most beautiful voice. "Because we don't need to."

Anne thought for a moment as she looked back to Abdiel who asked, "Would you like me to describe to you your light?"

Anne thought for a moment. She never cared for religion and didn't refer to herself as a Christian, but in just over a day she had witnessed firsthand the love of God and the devotion of the guardians.

She shook her head. "No, I'm good."

Abdiel was so proud of Anne and how far she'd come after what she had endured in her life. "They will say things, they will throw curses and try to harm you in ways no other can, but they cannot harm a child of God."

Rahim moved to the window, his large, armored frame looking awkward as he crouched down to peer through.

"Their hosts can however harm your physical body and I am quite certain Father has other plans for you," he said as he turned around and smiled. "Azazel is here, and he has Kokabiel and Zaqiel with him."

Anne looked at Abdiel.

"Azazel? He's the one from last night! Who is with him?" Anne moved to the window to see three shadowed male figures standing across the street.

She then looked at Rahim.

"And why are you smiling?"

"What's going on?" William asked as to he and Father Daniel, Anne looked to be having a conversation with herself.

"Just a minute," Anne said to William, who shrugged as he moved to Father Daniel. "Is there any other way out of here? Any windows or…"

William led the priest into the main hall as he searched for possible routes of escape.

Abdiel looked at Anne.

"Azazel is a fallen archangel along with his brothers Kokabiel and Zaqiel. They are very powerful, beyond either of us," he said as he looked between Rahim and Yelena.

Before any doubt or fear crept in Anne, the guardian continued.

"The reason my brother is smiling is…"

Rahim excitedly jumped directly in front of Anne. "The reason I am smiling little one is that I have never been in a battle such as this!"

Anne leaned around the large angel to look at Abdiel, who also began to smile. "Anne, we wouldn't take on a fallen angel alone."

At that moment William and Father Daniel walked back to join

Anne, who was trying to grasp what Abdiel was saying. All three Angels held hands and prayed in a tongue that she did not understand except for three names that stood out. Uriel, Raphael, and... Michael.

In a moment three portals of intense light filled the room so brightly that Anne had to shield her eyes. Slowly, each light dissipated into the shape of an Angel.

Raphael was the first Anne saw his armor was a bronze color that held the scratches of previous battles. He had matching scale armor that stopped just above his knees. He wore high-scaled boots and bracers that looked as if they were made by human hands. His skin was a beautiful oaken color, and he had short, cropped hair that held light brown highlights.

Uriel was the next Anne saw. She was the epitome of beauty as she wore flowing white robes and a golden chest plate adorned with symbols that Anne did not know. Her hair was a flowing Auburn that curled as it went down her back. She had a half helmet tiara on that was made of gold and crystal.

Anne slowly lifted her head to the final archangel.

Michael materialized directly in front of Anne, but with his back to her. Even from behind, he looked exactly like he did in the paintings. He was tall, with shoulder-length blonde hair that fell under a golden-winged helmet. His gilded chest armor was sleeveless and perfectly fit around his large, magnificent wings. His physique looked as if it had been chiseled from marble with tanned and toned muscles. He had no armor skirting like

Raphael, but a pure white tunic with gold trim that fell to his knees. Anne could see the back of his muscled calves, each of which had two leather straps from his golden shin armor.

"Did you feel that?" Father Daniel asked as he looked at William.

William lifted his forearm to see the hair standing on chill bumps. "Yeah, I definitely feel that! Anne, what just happened?"

Anne watched as Michael turned around to face her. His hair moved as if a breeze blew while his face, was that of an angel. He was no doubt masculine in every way, but he carried a softness in his smile that exuded pure love.

"Hello," his voice sounded pure, there was no accent to speak of.

His speech was perfect, but his voice sounded... more human.

"Hi," Anne said as she was awestruck by the angels around her.

"Anne! What... who do you see?" William asked excitedly.

Michael looked over. "Well, you better tell them before they burst," he said smiling, they were all smiling.

Michael, Raphael, Uriel, Rahim, Yelena and Abdiel.

Anne looked to Father Daniel and William, smiling so much her cheeks hurt. "Three more Angels just arrived."

Anne looked at them unbelievingly, feeling Father's love flow.

"Uriel, Raphael, and Michael."

Father Daniel crossed himself. He didn't know how but he already knew before she spoke. William smiled intently.

Anne looked to her right to see the hoard of demons standing just off the cathedral grounds led by the fallen Angels then she looked down overcome with grief.

Feeling this, Abdiel spoke up. "What is wrong, Anne? Are you not comforted?"

Anne raised her head. "Oh no, there are hundreds of demons here and I have never felt more comforted."

Tears flowed from her eyes as she bowed her head.

Michael used his incredible power to cross worlds for just a moment as he softly wiped a tear from Anne's face. "Then why do you weep so?"

Electricity flowed through Anne's body as she looked up, holding her cheek where Michael touched her.

She looked into his eyes that shone like blue diamonds. "Because I don't deserve you, any of you. I never believed. I haven't done anything good in this world. There are others, more deserving, more faithful who ne-"

Michael stood tall as he interrupted Anne.

"You are mistaken. You look at us as higher than you and *that* is where you are wrong. We are all God's children special in our own way," he leaned down slightly closer to her. "You, Anne, are our sister and are no less special than any other."

Uriel stepped forward. "We are not here for them," she said as she pointed outside.

Raphael was the next to move forward to within arm's reach.

"We are here for our sister!" he said as he smiled.

Abdiel looked at Anne, proud as a parent and loving as a brother. "And we fight with all that we are to defend our family."

Anne shook her head as tears flowed. "This is not fair. Like, I need to hug you guys!"

All six Angels surrounded Anne, filling her with more love than she ever imagined existed.

"I'm losing my mind," William said jovially. "I feel like I'm missing so much here."

Father Daniel nodded in agreement. "You too, huh?"

"We can take care of the demons, but you and William need to find a way out and away from their servants," Abdiel said as he turned to the task at hand.

Yelena pointed in the direction of the alter. "Remind Daniel about the basement window in the storage room, that is your best chance to escape."

Anne looked at Father Daniel. "Yelena told me to remind you about the basement window?"

Father Daniel looked back, confused. "Who?"

Anne's eyes got big. "Oops, not sure if I was supposed to tell you that, oh well, no putting that back in the bottle. Yelena is your guardian angel."

"Oh, well please tell her, thank you," the priest said unsure of how to respond to that information.

Michael turned to Abdiel, Raheem, and Yelena.

"Go with your wards, there is no demon that can stand against the three of you," Michael said reassuringly.

The archangel then turned slowly to look out the window. Michael's demeanor began to change. The smiling angel of love slowly faded and was replaced with the warrior angel of God's wrath. "We will deal with our fallen brethren."

Chapter 6: Spiritual warfare

"It's over here, behind these shelves!" Father Daniel said as he, William, and Anne pushed boxes and junk out of the way.

Everything was covered in a thick layer of dust, and the air smelled of mildew from the Louisiana humidity. William's jeans held a thick layer of dirt and grime he received moving a very old bike out of the way. He went to help Father Daniel move the shelves.

"Anne," Abdiel called.

Anne turned to look at the angel. He looked at her a bit sternly as he wanted her to heed his words, "The demons cannot step foot on consecrated ground but as soon as we leave the grounds, they will accost us."

He moved closer, looking Anne in the eyes. "It will be much worse than last night. We will be overwhelmed by their numbers. We will fight them off but yo-"

Anne interrupted the guardian.

"But they can't hurt me, and no matter how much they try to torment me, I won't give them any power over me," Anne stepped forward with a subtle smile.

She looked from Abdiel to Rahim and Yelena.

"I trust you."

Few things sadden an Angel more than when their ward loses faith, and nothing fills them with joy more than when one has it.

The three guardians smiled as their hearts were filled with Anne's faith in them.

"Okay, it looks clear. Let's go!" William said as he climbed out the small window first assessing the area.

Father Daniel grabbed Anne's hand and began helping her out the window when she paused.

"What's wrong?" he asked as Anne looked at the countless demons waiting just over the property lines only a hundred feet away.

"Nothing," Anne said with resolve as she continued her climb out of the window.

Once there, she turned around to give Father Daniel a hand.

He waved her on. "I've got to stay here, you two go while you have time!"

William heard this and turned around, but before he could protest the priest spoke up. "Go! It's only a matter of time till they get tired of waiting."

William nodded, turned, and grabbed Anne's hand then made their escape. The three angels had for the moment disappeared from Anne's sight. As she moved to within feet of the consecrated grounds boundary, she stopped, overwhelmed by the sounds she was hearing. Lines of demons from every level of hell formed ranks that seemed impenetrable. They moaned and screamed at her with profanities. Their movement sounded like millions of worms crawling all over. They breathed in quick, heavy bursts, excited as their prey neared.

Horns, scales, burned flesh, and gnashing teeth stood within just an arm's length of Anne as she snarled back with a smile.

"Y'all are about to get kicked right in your demon as-"

"This way!" William said as he pulled Anne forward through the crowd of demons that only she could see.

* * *

Michael, Raphael, and Uriel appeared only yards away from Azazel, Kokabiel, and Zaqiel. Michael walked forward fearlessly to face the fallen angels and well over a thousand demons. As he neared Azazel the demons behind him moved back in fear of the mighty archangel, even Azazel seemed to lean back instinctively.

"All we want is the girl's brother. You know that she will belong to us eventually as the light-bringer has commanded." Azazel said in fake confidence, "You can't keep us all from her."

Azazel waited for Michael's dramatic oration that he had tirelessly heard the archangel spew for millennia, but it did not come.

Michael stood filled with God's anger that they would so blatantly pursue one of his children. Fire filled the archangel's eyes as a shield of light appeared in his left hand and the sword of truth in his right. Unlike any other weapon, the sword of truth was created and given to Michael by God himself. It looked like a silver sword with a broad blade that was thinner at the hilt. Different from the usual light weapons used in spiritual combat, the sword of truth looked ornate, but human-made except for the bright white glow that emanated from its edge.

Raphael materialized a glorious angelic bow in his left hand while Uriel a long double-bladed staff that seemed to spark with flecks of golden light.

Michael's muscles flexed as he spoke through gritted teeth. "*You* are not my brother!"

Just as his sword arm moved back, two beings swooped down behind Raphael and Uriel. The two turned to face them as Michael turned just enough to regard Jomjael and Batarel, two more fallen angels.

Michael turned back to Azazel, who grinned. "So, how many of you is father willing to commit? Would you call more of your brothers and sisters away from their tasks to save this *one*? How many die, Michael, for every moment you are here?"

Azazel's body began to grow as darkness swirled around him. The man began to disappear as huge leathery wings grew from his back. His black eyes glossed over as his skin changed from that in God's image to that of a large, muscled hell beast. He stood over Michael and spoke as two lower fangs protruded over his upper lip. Every word uttered was a vile growl spewed in the archangel's direction.

"How many is your father willing to sacrifice, a thousand? Ten thousand? A hundred thousand?" Azazel laughed as he knew he was right.

Every moment the archangel's spent there, lives were lost somewhere else as Lucifer's forces corrupted and warped the minds of men.

A giant longsword proportionate to Azazel's beastly form materialized in his hand. The fallen angel looked down again.

"You cannot stop us, brother."

A small smile crossed Azazel's face as he lifted his sword and laughed. "We are legion!"

* * *

Anne closed her eyes as William guided her, opening them momentarily to see a handful of demons and ash flying through the air, lifted by mighty Rahim's speared chains. Unable to close them again, she watched the three guardians battle around her.

Yelena stayed with William and Anne and was as deadly as she was beautiful. She held a bladed disk in each hand with leather grips on one side and slightly curved points on the other. She moved with grace as she alternated between slashing and throwing her discs. Anne was in awe as each blade penetrated several demons, taking a wide swirling arc they cut through more upon returning to the angel's hand as she seamlessly caught one. She would turn and throw another.

Rahim moved like a whirlwind, his braided hair and sash flowing. Lines of demons were cut down like a tornado through a forest. Occasionally the guardian would pause long enough to throw the bladed tip forward, impaling all in its path.

Abdiel was the closest to Anne, directly in front of her and William. He was almost too fast to see as he teleported from one demon to the next, materializing every weapon in his arsenal. In one sequence the Angel sliced a demon to his right, spun to throw several light shards to his left then dematerialized only to return behind two demons a wrist blade piercing the neck and head of each.

Anne was so caught up in the spiritual battle she didn't see the three men turn the corner directly in front of them.

William didn't hesitate as he tackled the first, launching him into his partner. The third man immediately kicked at him, but he caught his foot and pushed him back into the nearby building.

"She's here, southwest corner!"

One of the tackled men yelled into his radio as William dropped on top of him to rain down strikes to the thug's face.

Anne didn't know what to do as she crouched close to the building, as she could barely see three feet in front of her through the spiritual battle around her.

The first man had rolled off to the side and drew a gun from his hip. William moved outside of his arm grabbing the gun with two hands and twisting the man's arm back over his shoulder disarming him and kicking him away. William then fired two shots at the man he threw against the building earlier before getting shot from behind.

The shots rang through Anne's ears as she heard Rahim scream above all the fighting.

"No."

Through the chaos around her, Anne could see William fall to the ground. She crawled over to him as fast as she could, but before she got there she was pulled by her hair from behind.

Sebastian forced her head back as he looked in her face. "I hope you're worth all this trouble."

He dragged Anne by her red hair. She screamed as two more men approached.

"Bring the..." Sebastian turned and hit Anne over the head with the butt of his pistol, knocking her out and shutting down her screams.

He let her fall to the ground as he ordered his lackeys. "Bring the van around now."

Junior had never been around a murder in public before and was extremely anxious. "Sheriffs gonna be pissed you killed the man."

Sebastian moved to Junior. "How many times do I have to tell you? I only serve one master."

Three shots rang like thunder.

* * *

Spiritual warfare is a sight to behold. Thousands of demons joined Azazel and his fallen brethren on the street in front of the cathedral. Though none passing could see it every man, woman, child, or animal that passed the battleground could feel the energy.

Demons swarmed the archangels from all sides. Raphael's angelic arrows rained like meteor strikes, each one exploding into sparks upon impact turning groups of demons to ash. Uriel spun her duel bladed staff with elegance and precision, cutting through swaths of demons in between her duel with Zaqiel and Jomjael. Her blade sliced the top of Jomjael's leg as she twirled low, but his skin was too thick. She immediately rolled to the side to dodge the incoming strike from Zaqiel's fiery spiked flail.

Batarel, Kokabiel, Azazel, and a host of demons all focused on the mighty Michael and still, they struggled. Michael charged forward with his shield so fast he was a blur as demons flew like swatted flies. The archangel turned in a wide swing, the light from the sword of truth extending the weapon's range dramatically as it cut through twenty demons. Using the momentum and sensing the large Azazel behind him, Michael swung up and down over the fallen angel. Sparks flew as Azazel blocked the blow with his large sword, but the force brought him to his knees. Unfortunately, Michael had no time for a follow-up attack as he spun to throw several demons back into Kokabiel. He then in a split second charged forward, moving through time and space to pierce Batarel in the shoulder. The blade of truth stung the fallen angel as it pierced through what would have been his heart had he not moved as fast as he did.

Fear instantly overwhelmed Batarel as he knew that mark would never heal. When defeated, angels return to the arms of Father while demons and fallen returned to hell, however, one who is cut down by the sword of truth simply ceases to exist.

Demons jumped on Michael as Azazel and Kokabiel grabbed his wings. Michael crouched low for a moment before taking flight in a burst of wind, breaking the clouds above. His foes looked up for that second in wonder before the warrior angel struck the ground hard enough to leave cracks in the road of the material world. The shock waves sent every demon and fallen angel flying fifty feet or more back.

Slowly and resiliently, Michael stood as he was joined by Raphael and Uriel once more. The fallen angels too began to rise with their demon army.

Azazel smiled as he looked at Michael. "Is that it?"

He and the fallen angels then disappeared as a hundred thousand demons descended upon the archangels.

* * *

The shots woke Anne from unconsciousness with a splitting headache. She reached behind her head to feel a bit of blood and a knot forming. Her first sights were of Sebastian limping away as fast as he could with a lot of blood gushing from the back of his thigh. She looked over to see several bodies lying on the ground and William on his side. He met her eyes for a moment before falling back to the ground, dropping the pistol.

"William!" Anne cried as she ran to him. "No, no, no!"

Anne tried to put pressure on the bullet wound that exited William's stomach, but there was just too much blood.

He looked up at her through ragged breaths.

"Take it... Run!" he said, motioning toward the gun.

Anne cried as she pulled William's head in her arms. "No, no, you can't die on me. You're all I have in this world!"

William wanted to speak, wanted to tell Anne how strong she was, how beautiful she was. He wanted to tell her what he'd been feeling since they met, how being with her felt familiar, like being home, and he wanted to tell her how sorry he was that he couldn't protect her. But he couldn't say anything more, as darkness closed in around him.

Anne sobbed as she felt William's life slipping away. She cradled him in her arms, not thinking of the danger around her... and then she looked up.

Abdiel and Yelena stood fighting as Rahim knelt by William's side, weeping, ready to take him home. Demons flooded in from everywhere, overwhelming them.

Azazel and his fallen Angels appeared instantly. Kokabiel, Zaqiel, Jomjael, Batarel along with two more Azza and Uzza.

Rahim charged at the large Azazel, whipping his bladed chain with his right hand. Azazel allowed the chain to wrap around his forearm and although the divine weapon burned his flesh, he endured as he yanked Rahim to him. Azza crushed Rahim in midair with his club sending him on his back. He and Uzza then began beating the twiceborn angel.

Yelena jumped in the air towards Azazel with her dual blades but was swatted to the side with enough force to severely injure.

Abdiel was furious, and he showed no fear as he teleported behind Kokabiel to slash at his ankle. He then threw a handful of light shards at Azza and Uzza before teleporting again into a downward strike upon Azazel who caught the guardian by the throat.

Abdiel grabbed at the large beasts' arms, flailing as he tried to escape.

Azazel smiled through his jagged teeth as he looked to Abdiel. "I remember you, little slave."

Azazel then squeezed tightly before throwing Abdiel like a rag doll.

Anne closed her eyes as she cried, cradling William in her arms. She rocked back and forth in sobs until a light shone so brightly it blinded her through her closed eyes.

Anne opened her eyes and couldn't make out anything at first, then she saw the shape of a man with his back to her. The fallen angels slowly backed up while the demons turned to flee, disappearing sporadically as they made their escape.

Slowly Anne was able to see the man take form. His robes were simple and flowing. His brown hair was wavy and messed about. As he slowly lifted his hand, his robe fell back, revealing where the nail had pierced his flesh.

As Jesus lifted his hand, the fallen moved to flee, but it was too late. With his palm outward a great pulse of light emanated from the Lamb, instantly turning the fallen angels and demons to ash, sending them back to the depths of hell.

In an instant, all was quiet except for Anne's sobs. Jesus turned to her with love and compassion in his eyes as he felt her pain. He slowly walked to kneel across from her next to William.

Anne cried uncontrollably as she looked into the eyes of the Lord. "Please, please, help him."

Jesus slowly reached his right hand to Anne's cheek, which instantly brought her an overwhelming feeling of calm and peace. She didn't know how but, she somehow knew that everything was going to be okay.

Jesus smiled slightly before placing his hands over William's wounds. Rahim, Yelena, and Abdiel recovered by Jesus's light, knelt around William, and joined the Lamb as he prayed.

"Father, even now your wonders amaze me. Your guidance is like that of a strong river, though the waters may sometimes be rough we know that you will lead us to our destination," Jesus paused as he looked up. "Father through you I heal this man so that he may serve your will, so that he and Julianne may continue on the journey you have for them."

Jesus grabbed Anne's hand as he met her eyes. "So that their children may serve your will as they fight the wickedness of this world."

The words had barely registered in Anne's brain when she felt the steep rise of William's chest. "William! William!"

The blood had stopped, and William's breathing had intensified. Jesus placed his hand on Anne's and gave a gentle squeeze.

"You two must leave this city," Jesus turned his eyes momentarily to the Angels. "Your guardians will guide you as they always have."

The Lamb stood, and Anne could tell he was about to leave. "No, wait!"

She looked up at Jesus with so many questions. Why did Father give her this gift? What did the fallen angels want with her? What was she supposed to do?

She wanted to at the very least tell the Lord, thank you, but she was only able to get three words to cross her lips, "I love you."

Jesus smiled wide as his sun-kissed cheeks wrinkled up to his eyes. "And I love you, Anne."

With those last words, the Lord stood and disappeared into a glow of beautiful bright light.

William immediately opened his eyes and shot up. "Wha... What happened?"

Anne wiped tears from her cheek as she laughed and looked into William's blue eyes.

"So much," she took a breath. "C'mon, we have to get out of here."

William lifted his shirt and wiped the blood away to see a healed scar on his stomach where a bullet hole was moments before. "What the hell?"

Anne pulled him up. "Come on, I'll explain later, but we have to go."

William quickly found his footing as he and Anne made their way down the alley. Yelena returned to Father Daniel while Rahim and Abdiel stayed close by their side. As they made their escape, the events played through Anne's mind over and over again. The love she felt from Jesus, the miracle, but mostly the words he said as he looked into her eyes.

* * *

So that their children may serve your will as they fight the wickedness of this world.

The Beginning

About the Author

As a child, I would sometimes watch Unsolved Mysteries with my parents, I guess that's really where it all began. My interest in UFOs, cryptozoology, and the paranormal have been with me all my life but for as long as I can remember, I've always looked at them differently. Before I was ten, I remember doing research, checking out books, articles and any material I could get my hands on. By my teens that focus had changed to researching faith and spirituality. After high school, I entered the Marine corps where my research into religion inevitably led me to secret societies. I've done enough research on the subjects to fill a library with a particular study into religion and secret societies. After the Marines, I took more of an interest in fiction and came across "The Davinci Code." I had previously read all the source material that author Dan Brown used for his books and thought I'd give it a try. This is when my thoughts turned to writing, using all my previous research and weaving my own stories around it! I love creating stories and characters! Along with my current project, I have plans for a series centered around aliens, and a series with a completely new take on the Vampire/

Werewolf genre. I look forward to working with Private Dragon to bring my worlds and characters to life!"

You can connect with me on:

🌐 https://privatedragon.com

Also by Anthony J Santora

Nathan Turner and the New World Order

They've taken away our freedom, lying to us for years as they methodically took our rights. They've sewed segregation, division and hatred, making us focus on what we are, while loosing sight of who we are. They've infected our bodies with viruses and drugs while poisoning our food to make us reliant on prescription medications. They've taken our children, sacrificed millions and manipulated generations more and still thats not enough. They wont stop until we submit completely to their will.

But some of us do not bend the knee so easily.

I knew this was coming, I...saw it. I don't know if we can win, I don't know if we can ever take back what was lost but there are two things I do know without question. Right here right now is where I am supposed to be... and it is also where you are supposed to be.

If you come with us I can't promise you safety, I can't promise that you won't go hungry, I can't promise that you will live, but I can promise that you will be free.

My name is Nathan Turner and I can't do this alone but together we can push back these evil ones and their New World Order.

Are you ready to fight?